MORE
of the BEST

MORE
of the BEST

Stories for Girls

Edited by

N. Gretchen Greiner

Illustrated by

Fred Irvin

Cover by

Olindo Giacomini

 GOLDEN PRESS
Western Publishing Company, Inc.
Racine, Wisconsin

Contents

It Takes All Kinds
of Girls

to make a book of stories for girls. That's because variety is the spice of a collection like *More of the Best*. As you read it, you'll find yourself watching the girls in these eleven different situations and seeing how each one manages to set things in motion to alter her life. More important, you'll discover that particular kinds of girls are beset by particular kinds of troubles—and you'll be impatient with the ones who don't realize that and change their ways.

You'll laugh *with* some of the girls and *at* some of them, and you may shed a quiet tear or two for others. You may even learn something about the way you yourself run the business of being a girl.

One thing is certain—you'll be intrigued as you share a significant piece of living with each of the girls in this book. Meet them all now. . . .

SHELLEY—casual, nonconforming, "liberated." Then, on a day that starts out just like any other day, she and Don go for a bike ride. . . .

CHRISTY tries borrowing a personality, as she would a necklace or a book, and it even works—for a while. But it's amazing how a lot of blistered fingers can bring out the best in a girl!

ANGELA thinks her parents' divorce is too much for her to bear—until someone whose loss has been far more tragic shows her that happiness is, after all, just a state of mind.

CONNIE, because a particular boy is on hand the particular night her cat has kittens, changes her mind fast about people being stereotypes. She realizes that, worst of all, she has even tried to make a stereotype of herself!

MARTHA learns a simple but disturbing truth: A harmful promise is better broken than kept. When keeping her friend's shabby secret makes Martha, too, a part of the shabbiness, it's time for some *unromantic* second thoughts.

CARRIE understands everyone else's problems, but when her own family begins to fall apart, she has no answers. For one terrible evening, however, necessity makes Carrie's cool competence answer enough.

FLAVIA figures a little voodoo is okay if it's for everyone's good; but when she tries it to find a wife for her widowed father and it really works—that's pretty spooky!

ANN can't stand up to her beautiful and popular cousin to avoid constant humiliation, but when that humiliation threatens the boy she cares for, Ann's courage is magnificent.

MEG, TRISH, AND KIX live through the horror of a dinner party that should happen only in a slapstick comedy. Still, observing a suitor in such a nightmare situation can be helpful!

JESSICA, just to please her friend, agrees to try her friend's various formulas for attracting boys. Nothing works, until suddenly, with the *right* boy, she finds herself doing all the *right* things—just naturally.

SARA has problems with her mother, who is poor but snobbishly ambitious for both Sara and herself. When Sara brings home the much-hoped-for "rich boy," her mother gains new insight into the really important things in life.

So—those are the scenes you'll be part of as you share each girl's life. Turn the page and enjoy *More of the Best!*

N.G.G.

A Different Kind of Knowing

Kay Haugaard

ROLLING OVER on her hastily made bed, Shelley balanced her book on her chest and, holding one leg high in the air, let her shoe slip off her foot until it hung from her big toe. She kept the shoe thus precariously dangling as she read, enjoying the subtle suspense of its possible fall.

Just being able to read something other than a dull assignment made Saturday a big relief. The book, entitled *Heredity and You,* fascinated her. She was engrossed in a chart showing that dark hair and eyes were dominant and light hair and blue eyes were recessive . . . that the children of blond, blue-eyed parents would be blond and blue-eyed . . . that children of dark-haired, dark-eyed

13

parents could possess almost any hair color or eye color, since recessive genes for lightness of hair and eyes could be carried by dominantly dark parents.

"Shelley! Don's here to see you." Shelley became vaguely aware of her mother's calling.

She stopped reading just long enough to shout, "I'm in the bedroom, Mom." Then she resubmerged in her book and speculations, whirling her shoe quickly on her big toe, as though the quickening in her brain demanded a comparable physical activity.

There it was, as beautiful as anything: the opportunity for a scientific experiment! Her dog, Frosty, was all white. If she were bred to another all white, the pups would be all white, right? But if, on the other hand— A new, complicating thought came to her, and she reached out for another book from the shelf: *Practical Dog Breeding*.

Just think! She could start a whole new breed of dog, the all white German shepherd. She thumbed past chapters that dealt with the mechanics of mating, care during gestation, and the whelping process, until she came to "Heredity—a Brief Examination." She read quickly, absorbing the information she needed.

Suddenly her mother appeared at the bedroom door. "Shelley, didn't you hear me? Don is here. He wants to know if you'd like to go for a bicycle ride."

"Just a sec, Mom."

The fact that Don had come over was hardly a reason to stop two pages from the end of the chapter. She saw Don every day in school. He was like a brother. He was a friend, not a boyfriend. Shelley liked to talk to him and argue with him about just any old thing, but he certainly wasn't worth her not finishing the chapter.

As she left the doorway, Shelley's mother said in a low voice, "Shelley, don't be so rude."

So, when she came to the end of the paragraph, she shouted, "Come on in, Don."

Don came striding into the room on his long legs, his white T-shirt too tight around his chest, as though it had shrunk—or he had grown. "Hey, what's this?" He was looking at a brightly lighted tropical fish aquarium whose background was painted with a brilliant turquoise crystallizing solution. There were two black-barred angelfish swimming about sedately, while four little neon tetras alternately darted and glided around the tank in flashily choreographed counterpoint.

The shoe Shelley was dangling dropped suddenly, thumping down uncomfortably onto her stomach. She lowered her book for a moment and asked, "Didn't I have that last time you were here? I've had it almost a month. Not many fish, but look at the snails! I got a few from the canal, and they're reproducing as if they want to populate the world. They're some kind of family types, I guess." She lifted the book to her face and continued to read.

Don picked up the things on the desk with a jaded air; he had seen them many times before. He picked up her drawing board and examined a fish design she had started. "What's this, a wallpaper pattern for a john?"

"Will you stop asking questions and interrupting? I'm almost through with this chapter; then we'll go. Look at my rock samples while you're waiting. I got them up by the quarry."

Don started poking around the desk for the rock samples, and Shelley eagerly finished the chapter. Then, sitting up quickly, she started to tell Don about the book. She tossed it to him to look at and rummaged around in a drawer for a comb.

"Of course, Frosty is too young to breed yet. I think I'll wait another season."

Now Don flopped on the bed and started to read

while she combed her hair and anchored her silver barrette in place. "Did you get the calf for 4-H?"

Don was already lost in the book. "Huh? No, but I've got one started."

"Started?"

"Dad lent me the fifty-dollar stud fee for Bellingham's Pride. He's the best bull in the northwest. Sired twice as many champions as any other bull."

"So you got Pansy serviced?"

"Yup."

"Hey, that's wonderful." Shelley snatched her red sweater from the closet so quickly that the metal hanger twanged back and fell off the pole. "Where'll we ride?" As she walked out of her room, Don rose from the bed and followed.

Don moved through the kitchen, past Shelley's mother, out the back door, and down the porch steps in what seemed like three strides. Shelley was putting a banana and half a slightly stale jelly roll in a sack, when her mother spoke to her, very softly, after first glancing around to see if Don was well out of hearing.

"Shelley, I *wish* you would stop inviting Don into your room like that. You are not a child anymore. I should think you'd start acting like a young lady."

Shelley's hand stopped in midair, as though

17

struck with paralysis. Surely her mother couldn't have meant that the way it sounded. "Mom! What a funny thing to say. What's wrong with it? Don's my *friend!*" She accented the word "friend" as though it contained a complete and irrefutable explanation. Then, angrily, she pushed open the screen door and swung down the steps to where Don waited, already astride his bike.

Of all the idiotic, ridiculous, dopey notions! she raged to herself. *Where did Mother get such a crackpot, archaic idea? So it's some kind of silly convention that a boy isn't supposed to come into a girl's bedroom. Well, it isn't just a bedroom; it's also a study and laboratory and library and hobby shop. If it happens to have a bed in it, too, what of it?* She ran her bike along the gravel driveway and jumped on, staring straight down and silently seething. What an old-fashioned attitude! Why, Don wasn't even someone who would tempt her in a car at night (she *guessed,* because she had never had an opportunity to be tempted in a car —or anywhere else, for that matter).

She stared into the bright sky, unseeing, brooding over her mother's remark. They were on the paved highway now, going toward the freight station beside the railroad tracks.

"Want to go to the station?"

"Looks like we're halfway there already!" Shelley answered rather sharply.

"What's eating you?" Don frowned as he gave her a quick look.

"Oh, nothing." And as suddenly as it had entered, her anger fled from her mind—forced out by the bright sun, the blue sky, the red gold bronco grass that was all dry-brushy-whispery with every air current, and the delicate balance of her bike as it seemed to propel itself along the flat, hard road. Taking her hands from the handlebars, she held her arms wide, feeling the cool autumn air rush past her, sending her hair streaming back. She grabbed the handlebars again, rose to a standing position, and pumped out ahead of Don like a flash.

"Race you!" She sailed ahead of him, with her red sweater flapping like a flag. She felt him gaining, and she could hear the hard, rhythmic pull of his tires and see his long, lean figure from the corner of her eye. She pedaled harder and harder, rocking her weight from side to side, jerking the handlebars alternately as the tires grabbed the road. Then he was speeding past her and far into the lead.

19

Shelley stopped pumping and sat back, resting, her feet idle on the pedals as the bike rolled along with a small, vibrating hum. Seeing that she would be beaten, she yelled, "Let's go to the potato cellars instead."

Don swung his bike around in a sharp arc, holding his foot out to brake and to brace himself if he started to fall.

She turned off on a dirt road, with a bump and a skid on the loose dirt that made her grip the handlebars more tightly. He was beside her in a moment, and they rode along side by side, silent, both too out of breath to talk. Her chest pounded, and the hot air seemed to force its way into her lungs, stinging them.

They rode along the wooden loading dock. It was like a boardwalk, about six feet above the ground. The boards ran lengthwise, and when her tire suddenly went into a groove, it nearly jerked the bike from her hands. A couple of times she felt a wrench, but she stiffened her grip and put on the brakes.

At the end of the dock there were loading ramps. The boards were laid across the width of the ramp. She touched her brakes a little and went clattering down. The boards rattled and vibrated all the way to the ground, where she shot off into one of the two green-fringed ruts that served as a truck road.

Shelley noticed that one of the cellars was open, and she rode into its cool darkness that smelled strongly and moistly of potatoes. She wondered if Don would notice where she'd gone. She stopped riding along the dirt floor and drew over into the dark, away from the slanting sunlight. She was glad for a little rest and stood on one foot, her other leg over the seat of the leaning bike. She was still breathing heavily.

She saw Don come speeding down the ramp. He turned sharply and stopped when he reached the bottom, looking from side to side. Seeing the open cellar, he rode slowly into it. She stayed quiet in the shadows until he had pedaled past her hiding place behind the big partition of a potato bin. Then she leaped out from behind him and yelled, "Boo!" He stopped the bike with a jerk and put out his leg to catch himself.

"Hey!" His pant leg was tangled in the chain, and he flung his arm out to balance himself. Shelley quickly grabbed the bike by the rear fender and steadied it. Don's arm came down around her shoulders before he leaned the bike the other way and stopped his fall with his unentangled leg.

Then he was balanced, with no need to lean on her, but his arm was still around her. In the preceding impulsive action, there had been no time for feeling, but now his arm around her shoulders felt strange and unnecessary. Looking up at his face, she saw her own feelings mirrored there. As their eyes met, she had a strange sensation—almost like fear. It was in his eyes, too.

She turned her head away and stood silent. His arm still rested across her shoulders like a dead thing. After a moment, she felt it tighten hesitantly, and his fingers encircled her arm. She laid her head against his chest and stood rigid, feeling uncertain and frightened. Then, almost against her will, she lifted both her arms and put them around him, raising her face to his. She saw the look of helplessness and alarm in his eyes before he bent and put his lips against hers—so lightly, so gently, and for just an instant.

"You're . . . you're . . . nice, Shelley." His voice sounded choked.

She drew back a bit and studied him. He seemed different. The planes of his thin face now had a sensitive look, and his lips, which she had thought too full, were finely chiseled, expressive. She took his hand and stood motionless for a moment, her

eyes on the rough, wheel-scarred ground of the cellar. She felt confused and dizzy and wonderful. She didn't want to leave, but she said, "We'd better go. It's kind of chilly in here."

It was warmer in the sunlight, and she tied her red sweater around her waist before they started for home, pedaling slowly, riding hand in hand much of the way, even though it was awkward. Sometimes one or the other would swerve and they'd lose their balance. Then they'd laugh and drop hands, but just for a moment. Before they came too close to her house, Don stopped his bike and pulled Shelley to a stop. He kissed her again, but this time he held her for a longer time, and she didn't want him ever to let her go.

As they rode into the gravel driveway, Don said, "How about lending me that book you were reading . . . about heredity?"

Shelley understood that he was just casting about for something to say. It was difficult for her, too, to force her attention back to things of the everyday world, but she answered, "Sure, you can borrow it." She tried to bound up the steps in her usual self-possessed manner, but she moved stiffly and clumsily, acutely conscious that the heat of her

24

cheeks had nothing to do with riding her bike in the hot sun.

She went into the house, and Don followed, carefully closing the door behind him.

"It's right in my bedroom, Don," she said, hurrying toward her room, with Don at her heels. At the end of the hall, in front of her door, they both stopped short and looked at each other with sudden embarrassment.

Shelley's eyes moved from Don to the doorway, then back to Don. She laughed nervously. "I'll go get it," she said and went into her room, leaving Don waiting quietly in the hall.

Not Many Girls
Play First Bass

Lael J. Littke

WHEN I HAVE a problem to think through, I like to
drape myself around my big bass fiddle and saw
out doleful dirges while I plan what to do. I've
spent a lot of time playing that bass during the past
couple of years. When you're shy to begin with,
then, at fourteen, shoot up to a height of five feet
nine inches, with size ten feet to trip over, that's
something of a problem right there. Hang wire-
rimmed glasses in front of your eyes and have hard-
ware installed on your teeth by the orthodontist,
and suddenly you feel like the Thing from Outer
Space. Who needs you? The only time people really see you is when they want to tease.

The kids in Linville teased me plenty. "Christy

Coleman, the girl who plays first bass," they called me. It started when I was promoted to the first chair in the bass section of our school orchestra, but it sounded as if I were the queen of sandlot baseball. That was good for more laughs, because they knew that, to me, baseball was an unexplored wilderness.

Things weren't too good there in Linville, but when Dad announced that his company was transferring him to a new town, I really had a problem to think about. Mom gave me her Lecture Number Thirty-Seven: "Things Are Never as Bad as They Seem." It didn't help. Things were *easily* as bad as they seemed. How could I, Christy Coleman, girl disaster, face a move to a new place, where I didn't know a single soul? At least, the kids in Linville were used to me.

I was playing "The Volga Boatmen" on Boris—that's what I call my bass—and my tears were flowing freely over his bridge on the day when I figured out what to do. I wouldn't go to our new home in Stonington as Christy Coleman—not exactly. I would go as Marnita Lester, thinly disguised as Christy Coleman.

Marnita Lester was the most popular girl in our school. She was as homely as a plucked chicken, but she didn't let that bother her in the least. When she got a new blemish on her face, she just shrugged and said, "Who'll notice it among all the others?" Marnita was lively and fun—a laugh a minute. I was going to be like her, sweeping into Stonington as "Crazy Christy Coleman, the girl no party can be without."

I was going to retire Boris, too. No more "first bass player" for me!

We moved to Stonington in June, right after school was out. I arrived in town like a teen-age Totie Fields, armed with one-liners ("I'm so tall, I have to telephone my feet to move") and old riddles (Question: How do you catch a rabbit? Answer: Make a noise like a carrot).

When two girls and a tall, red-haired boy, all looking to be within a year or two of my age, came ambling along to watch the movers unload our furniture from the van, I started right in.

"Don't tell me," I said. "Let me guess. You're undercover agents for the FBI, checking us out for smuggled termites. . . . You're talent scouts looking for a dancing telephone pole. . . . You're the local vigilantes, and you've got a Not Wanted poster on me." My rapid-fire delivery would have done credit to Don Rickles.

The trio looked a little surprised, but then the boy grinned and said they had just stopped by to welcome us to Stonington. He introduced the three of them as Penny, Pat, and Larry. Penny and Pat were twins, and he was their older brother.

"Penny, Pat, and Larry," I rasped. "You sound like the successors to Peter, Paul, and Mary."

"Say, you're quick on the draw," Larry said.

I nodded. "Fastest jaw in the West, that's me."

This time Penny, Pat, and Larry laughed out loud. "You sure are," Penny said. "You're just what we need around here."

I congratulated myself, thinking it really wasn't too hard to be a reasonable facsimile of Marnita Lester—not when no one knew what the real Christy Coleman was like.

Stonington is a very small town, and it wasn't long before my fame as a comedienne had spread. The kids invited me to parties, and for a few weeks, I had a ball keeping everybody laughing. But somehow I didn't feel that I was one of them. I felt as if I were onstage, and if I stopped being funny, no one would bother to look at me.

Sometimes I really wanted to stop being funny, like the night Larry gave me a kind of puzzled look and said, "Christy, don't you ever have a serious thought in your head?" I liked Larry, and I wanted to sit down and talk to him about serious things—the government, community problems, what to do about college. If I did, he would realize that Christy Coleman was a fraud, that behind the jokes and the wisecracks was a shy bean pole whose face was made up of eyeglasses and stainless steel braces. So I said that I'd had a serious thought once, but it had almost short-circuited my brain. Larry smiled a little and went off to talk to someone else.

Somewhere along the line, I discovered that you can't take off the old personality and put on a new one the way you do a pair of jeans. As time went by, I ran out of jokes, and I became frantic trying to think up new ways to be funny. I put lampshades on my head and did silly dances—anything for a laugh.

But no one laughed much after a while. I had run dry of one-liners. I had recycled old jokes until they no longer inspired even a groan. I had made a big fool of myself so often that no one watched my performances anymore.

I guess I finally realized that my plan wasn't working the day Bill Felton, the City Recreation Director, held tryouts for a little show the Parks and Recreation Department sponsored every summer. All of us kids were gathered together in the little town park, where we liked to hang out, and Bill Felton was telling us about the show.

"The script is short, but it's funny," he said. "I know because I wrote it." He paused for the kids to laugh, then went on. "For the leading part, I need someone who's not necessarily short but who can be funny."

"Christy's funny," someone said, and there were a lot of laughs that sounded more like snickers.

"Do something funny, Christy," someone else said, and all eyes turned my way.

Desperately I tried to remember what Marnita Lester did that was funny. I recalled the time someone had thrown her little orange hat so far up in a tree that she couldn't get it down. She had put a sign on the tree; it said, "The Marnita Lester Orange Hat Memorial." Every day she would bring a little bunch of flowers to put beneath the tree in memory of her hat, and the kids had thought it was hilarious.

I looked around at all the faces turned toward me, and I saw in them more pity than encouragement. Stooping down, I took off my tennis shoes and threw them into the tree I was leaning against. Through suddenly trembling lips, I said, "This is

31

the Christy Coleman Shoe Tree."

The shoes fell right back down, and someone said sarcastically, "Wow, that's funny."

The only person who laughed was Larry, who said, "Pick your shoes from the Christy Coleman Shoe Tree." But even Larry couldn't save that dismal situation. The kids turned back to Bill.

I picked up my shoes, and when I thought no one was looking, I slunk off. "Christy," Bill called after me, "there's lots of singing and dancing in this show. We'll need you in the chorus."

"Singing gives me hives," I mumbled and went on home.

So I was right back to being dumb old Christy Coleman again, only it was worse here in Stonington than it had been in Linville, because the kids didn't even care enough to tease me. They just left me alone. The only ones I saw at all were Penny, Pat, and Larry, and that was because they lived right on the same street, and sometimes they went past my house when I was out watering the lawn or something. They said the rehearsals for the show were going well. Larry had the leading part. They asked a couple of times if I wouldn't come and help with the singing, but when I said no, they stopped asking.

I was so depressed about everything that I went back to playing Boris again, crying softly on his polished wooden shoulder.

I was playing a string bass version of Chopin's "Funeral March" one day, when the phone rang. Minutes later, Mom stuck her head into my room. "Bill Felton's on the phone," she said. "He's called to see if I'd help sew costumes for the show he's putting on. He also wants to know if what he heard in the background is a dying buffalo or a string bass. He wants to talk to you."

I didn't want to talk to him, but I knew if I didn't, Mom would deliver her Lecture Number Sixteen: "Do Something Active when You're Feeling Blue." I picked up the phone and said hello with all the enthusiasm that I usually save for my dentist. I didn't want Bill to know I played the bass. I didn't want to become known again as "Christy Coleman, the girl who plays first bass"— not on top of everything else.

"Christy," Bill Felton boomed, and I braced myself to say no. "Christy, I've been beating the bushes for a bass player. We need a combo for the show, and I've got Jack Dubriski on the guitar and Hal Taylor with his banjo. All I need is you with your string bass, and my problems are over. Come to rehearsal tomorrow night at the rec center, and bring your bass." There was a pause while he yelled encouragement to someone in the background. Then he said, "This is a big day, Christy. Larry's finally learned to tell his right foot from his left most of the time, and I've found a bass player. See you tomorrow night." There was a click as he hung up. I didn't even get a chance to refuse.

Well, what did it matter? Who would notice me behind Boris? Nobody looks at the bass player.

I expected some wisecracks when I came into the rehearsal hall with the big bass, and I wasn't disappointed. At first the kids looked at me kind of expectantly, waiting for me to do something silly. Then somebody yelled, "Where'd you get the big ukulele?"

Someone else answered, "That's no ukulele. That's a violin specially built for Christy!"

A few kids laughed, and there was an awkward silence that I was supposed to fill with a snappy answer, but I didn't say a word. I went to my music stand and looked at the notes Bill had written out for me. The kids shuffled around a little, but then the rehearsal went on, and no one said anything further to me.

The next few rehearsals were the same way. No

35

one even saw me anymore, and that was all right with me. I have to admit, though, that the show was fun. Some of the kids really had talent. Larry had a part something like Professor Harold Hill in *Music Man,* a fast-talking character who did some fancy footwork, too—or, rather, he was supposed to. Larry really did have trouble telling his left foot from his right, but when he made a mistake, he just laughed along with everyone else.

I began to enjoy being a part of the show, even though all I did was lurk there behind Boris, plucking out the bass notes.

But it seemed that Christy Coleman was destined not to be a part of anything, because it wasn't long until I developed big blisters on my fingers. It was getting close to the day of the performance, so we were rehearsing long hours, and since I hadn't played Boris much in the past several weeks, my fingers had softened. When you play a stringed instrument, you have to keep your fingers toughened, or they get sore. Mine got sore, all right— blisters not only on my left-hand fingers that held down the strings but also on the fingers of my right hand, because I was plucking the bass rather than using the bow.

When I showed Bill Felton and told him I

couldn't be in the combo, his shoulders slumped. "Gosh, Christy, I don't know how we'll get along without you."

I thought it was nice of him to say that, even though I knew they'd never miss me. The guitar and banjo could carry on just fine.

"Don't tell the kids why I'm not playing," I told Bill. I was afraid they would think it was just another crazy stunt. Bill agreed, after saying how sorry he was that I'd got the blisters.

When it came time for the next rehearsal, I couldn't stay away. Mom and the other costume ladies were working behind a screen at the back of the rehearsal hall, so I went there, saying I was going to help them. I really wasn't much help, though. My fingers were too sore to hold a needle, and besides, all I did was listen to what the kids were doing.

Larry was having a terrible time with his dance sequences. More than once, Bill Felton had to stop the rehearsal to tell him to think. "Larry! Which is your left foot? Start out with your *left foot*. The performance is two days off, and you still can't keep those big feet sorted out."

But Larry couldn't get it right. Finally he threw up his hands in exasperation. "Look," he said, "I can't keep those big feet sorted out unless I hear the beat—strong and steady. What happened to Christy? I need her thumping it out on that bass fiddle of hers!"

For a minute, I wondered if he'd said that just to get me involved again. I didn't think so. In the first place, I'm not sure he knew I was there. And in the second place, he wouldn't be fooling around, fouling up the whole show, just to coax me back. Larry truly needed Boris—and me.

I looked at my blistered fingers. If I wrapped them with several layers of tape, they probably wouldn't hurt too much. It wouldn't do my playing much good, but the notes were easy, and I could make the beat strong and steady.

"Mom," I said, "we have to go home and get my bass. Do you mind—please?"

The performance was almost perfect, and the audience clapped and cheered as if it were the best show they'd ever seen. I managed to do all right on Boris, even though, I must admit, my fingers still hurt pretty badly. I was glad no one noticed, though, because I didn't want any attention.

Backstage, after the show, Bill Felton compli-mented the cast. "Highest honors go to Larry," he said, "for starting on the right foot tonight. What I mean is, starting on the left foot, which is the right foot to start on."

Everyone was in high spirits, and there was a lot of laughter.

Larry stood up on a chair. "Full credit goes to our distinguished orchestra for giving me a steady beat," he said. "Let's hear it for the combo!"

The cast clapped.

"And most of all," Larry continued, "let's hear it for Christy, the girl who plays music to build blisters by."

So they had noticed my sore fingers. As the cast clapped again, I was embarrassed and would have faded quietly out the door, except that it's a little hard to fade quietly when you're lugging a bass fiddle. I looked around at the kids, and this time I didn't see any pity on their faces—only friendly grins. They continued to clap.

Suddenly I realized that they weren't giving me recognition just because I had pounded out a steady beat but because I had gone beyond what was expected of me, staying with the show despite my blistered fingers. It was good sportsmanship they were recognizing. It occurred to me that that was what the kids in Linville had liked about

Marnita Lester, too—not that she was funny but that she was a good sport all the time. I wished I had realized that sooner.

Bill Felton came up and clapped me on the back. "Sure glad to have you here, Christy. You're the first bass player to come to Stonington in a long time."

Then, of course, it was inevitable that someone should yell out, "Christy Coleman plays first bass!"

I didn't let it shrivel me, though, as I had back in Linville, and when Larry said, "Not many girls play first bass," I wound up and made believe I was throwing a ball at him. He pretended to catch it and yelled "*Out!*"

But I knew I wasn't out. I was in. Not as an unreasonable facsimile of Marnita Lester, either, but as Christy Coleman, five feet nine, wire-rimmed glasses, stainless steel braces, and all.

Larry came through the crowd of kids who were admiring Boris and picked up the big fiddle. "I'll carry this out to your car for you, Christy. You know, I've never before known a girl who played first bass."

"Funny thing is," I said, "I don't know a home run from an umpire!"

Larry grinned. "I'll teach you," he promised.

Sunday's Child

Audrey DeBruhl

UNEXPECTEDLY, after my brother Ned's graduation, we moved—away from Chicago and all the gang at school . . . Maribeth, my best friend . . . our handsome brick house on Wood Street . . . my father and our bittersweet Sundays together—away from all the things that had been my entire life.

It was Carson's idea. I pleaded, with tears, and I threatened that I would go to live with my real father. But Carson and Mother went right ahead making plans, anyway, arranging to sell the house and packing and selling household things. Carson had been granted a year's leave of absence from his engineering job, to write a book about aerodynamics or some other complicated thing. In the meantime, he and Mother would be running a motel in northern Florida, and we were going to live in it.

Too soon, we were there, and so there *I* was, dumped on the forsaken Gulf—not in the picture book part of Florida everyone imagines, either, but on a scraggly beach, in an old-fashioned, cement block apartment motel—with a long, dreary summer ahead of me. I just couldn't believe that my stepfather, who ordinarily was so kindhearted, could turn into such a thoughtless monster.

I brooded next to the pool that first day. It was a tiny, cramped little pool that no one but babies could like. It was surrounded on three sides by the wretched, fading walls of the motel. The fourth side was screened by a basket-weave fence that was supposed to be protection from the wind.

I was fourteen, and I thought, as I sat dangling my feet in the tepid water of the pool, that my life had already ended. I thought about the graduation and how lucky Ned was. His life had just begun.

Ned's graduation had been truly impressive. Ned wore a royal blue robe with a sweeping silver cowl, and everyone there seemed very solemn and kind of awed. Mother had bought a new dress for me, a dotted swiss A-line in pastel pink that made my brown hair look almost blond. It wasn't every day, she said, that one's brother graduated from high school.

Sure, I thought, and Ned was going to start summer school at the University of Illinois and didn't have to worry about moving to Florida. I guessed that the dress was supposed to make me forget that I couldn't go to school where *I* wanted to, the way Ned could, or even *live* where I chose.

Actually, I rather liked the graduation, because it helped shut out of my mind what was happening to me; so I wasn't prepared for that moment in the lobby afterward. We were standing there waiting for Ned—Mother, Carson, and I—when I saw my father standing near the door. It hit me, like a sudden blow to the stomach, that I wouldn't see him again for a whole year. A complete, entire, long year. We were leaving the next day, and he just stood there talking with some people, trying to act very ordinary and casual.

A great, unbearable pain rushed up from my insides—a fury of resentment that I couldn't hold back any longer. I heard myself screaming. It was loud and terrible, like something you might hear in a cheap horror movie. I clawed through the crowd, in a frenzy to reach my father. I grabbed his shoulders and pressed my teary face to his chest, leaving wet streaks on his blue suit. I probably even left some on the bright orange dress his girl friend was wearing.

Everyone stared, of course, and shock waves rolled through the crowd. I suppose I was more shocked than anybody.

All the way home in the car, no one said a word. It was dreadful. I crawled into bed that night hating myself. I could imagine what was going on inside all of them: Ned, his big moment spoiled; Mother embarrassed; Carson—well, I never could be sure what Carson was thinking. I did know that my father had looked both disgusted and humiliated as he pried me from his chest.

Then the bedroom door opened. Mother walked in and sat on the edge of my bed. "Why did you do that, Angela?" Her voice was very quiet.

Here it comes, I thought. *Why? Why do I do such crazy things?* I slid down a little under the covers. "I guess because of the way Dad looked."

"And how did he look?"

"Kind of, well, *sad*, I guess."

Mother sighed. "Angela, it's been three years. We're all trying to make a new life. It's been hard

44

on you, I know—the divorce . . . and then getting adjusted to a stepfather. But your father knows we're moving away, and he has accepted it. He wants you to visit him at Christmastime."

She kissed me softly and left. I felt terribly, terribly sorry. I always felt sorry after I did things. There had been other scenes about my father, other scenes just as stupid, and I didn't know why. I just knew I felt guilty and horrid.

Looking back, I do think it had a lot to do with Sundays. That was visitation day. I always got clammy when I'd see my father's blue station wagon pull up to our door, promptly at ten o'clock. That was the time to start pretending that everything was normal, when, inside, I felt torn to bits—because part of me wanted to go and part of me wanted to stay.

Then I'd feel just the same way about going home again, after supper at his apartment. Dad always seemed to try so hard to be fun to be with—and he never was. Nothing was the way it used to be, no matter how much we all tried to pretend. It bothered me that Ned didn't seem to mind the Sundays the way I did, but Ned didn't seem to leave a piece of himself at each house, either.

Every leave-taking, Dad would give me a kiss

45

and say, "You're all I have now, Angela, you and Ned." Then he'd get a cloudy look in his eyes and bite his lower lip, and we never knew what to say.

Not that Dad was cruel; he wasn't. But somehow he always had to say that, and it hurt inside me as I'd go up the front walk slowly, not wanting to look too eager to be back home. I couldn't escape the cold knowledge that I wouldn't have both parents anymore—not ever—and no amount of talking to myself, telling myself that this was life, seemed helpful. There was always another Sunday looming before me.

So, as I said, I sat brooding next to the pool, plunked down in that miserable place, wondering how I was going to get through the summer without Maribeth and the other kids I knew—without *anything* that was the least bit familiar.

Then I heard laughter from the beach, just a few yards away, beyond the fence. I listened for a while, and when the laughter didn't stop, I pulled my feet out of the water, then walked to the end of the fence to see what was so funny.

I saw two teen-agers in swimsuits, frolicking in the sand. The boy and the girl were both golden bronzed, lithe, and tall. The girl had very wet long blond hair, and the boy's dark curls, dripping, hung down to his eyebrows. They seemed to be playing a game without rules—or maybe rules that only they could understand—just running in and out of the water.

"Hey!" the boy called. "Are you the new girl at the motel?"

"Yes," I said.

"At last!" cried the girl. "My dear brother, we have an observer! I didn't think it would ever happen to us—that much luck!"

"I didn't mean to stare," I said stiffly. "I just heard the noise, and I—"

"No, no," said the girl, walking over to me. "I didn't mean it that way. I meant an observer for the boat. That's water-skiing language. It takes three; one to drive the boat, one to ski, and one to observe. Our dad gets tired of doing it. You know, *observing*. Watching the skier, in case he falls. It's the law. You have to have one."

"Oh, I see," I said, not seeing at all. Our place was on an isolated finger of sand, pointing out to the gulf. There wasn't a boat or a pier anywhere.

"Let's go tomorrow. You can meet us at our house. Ten o'clock, okay?" She pointed down the beach toward a squat pink house, the only one anywhere near our grubby motel.

"Okay," I said. I watched them run toward the pink house. They looked about as unalike as any brother and sister could. I guessed the girl to be fifteen or sixteen and the boy just a year or so older.

The pair played tag in my mind all the rest of the afternoon. I dusted the apartments, preparing for the guests we hoped would come. Our place had twenty apartments, stacked into three decks, with tiny balconies and outside stairways. Our apartment was at the bottom, nearest to the road, and just like all the others, except ours had two bedrooms instead of one.

That night at dinner, I mentioned that I had met some kids on the beach.

"That's wonderful, Angela," Mother said. "I'm afraid there aren't many young people around here."

"They must be the Ohlmstead children," Carson said.

"How do you know?" I asked. Carson always seemed to know more than he let on.

"The owner of this place told me about our neighbors when we were signing the lease." Carson had eyebrows that came together over his nose, and when he was pleased, the eyebrows shot up

48

high on his forehead. "I think you're going to like those youngsters."

I walked over to the pink house the next morning, carrying a towel from the motel and my sunglasses for observing. I wore last year's swimsuit, which was faded to a blur of tan and gray. Compared with the Ohlmsteads, I felt faded myself, inside and outside. Some kids had all the luck, I kept thinking.

I rang the bell. Immediately the boy and the girl popped out the door, laughing and chattering. They raced toward a queer-looking car parked on the oystershell driveway.

"Come on, Angela, get in," the boy called.

"What is it?" I asked. The thing was just motor, huge wheels, seats, and two hoops for a top. "And how do you know my name?"

"It's a beach buggy. And we know your name because we knew Mr. Katzman, who ran the motel before you. He nearly went broke."

"Oh," I said, climbing in next to the girl. I felt like someone from another planet.

"My name is Dorothy," the girl volunteered. "And don't worry about what Tommie said. Your father looks much smarter than Mr. Katzman." As Dorothy spoke, I studied her. *Vibrant* was the word I thought of. The clear, suntanned skin glowed with health, and the deep blue eyes, fringed with dark lashes, were lighted as if from inside.

"He's my stepfather," I said, wanting to get things straight.

"Oh, yes, I know that," Dorothy said lightly. "Do you know how to ski? We forgot to ask you yesterday."

The beach buggy roared like an airplane about to take off, so I just shook my head and grabbed the edge of the seat. There weren't any doors.

We zoomed down the road to the bridge that connected our strip of land to the town, then out to the highway. Wind streamed through my hair, and, oh, how I wished that Maribeth and the gang back home could see me!

Abruptly, Tommie turned off down a dirt road and then jerked to a stop in front of an old wooden boathouse that seemed about to tumble into the water.

"This is it!" Tommie jumped out and helped me down, then Dorothy. I followed them inside, where I saw an old beat-up motorboat suspended from two pulleys. Tommie quickly cranked it down into the water, explaining that the salt in the water would ruin the bottom of the boat, so they had to keep it pulled up.

"You look like you have good legs for skiing," Tommie said, hoisting a long, wide ski from a shelf. "I think you could learn real fast."

"Oh, no, I don't think so. I'd rather just watch. What do I do now?"

"Get in, and keep your eyes on Dorothy. Holler at me if she falls. That's what we need an observer for, because I have to look ahead, not back." He started the motor. "You can try later if you want to. It's easier to start with two skis, but we sold ours when we bought the slalom." He flashed a quick, bright smile. I thought that Tommie was the handsomest boy I'd ever seen.

I watched Dorothy, in her life belt, on the end of the pier as Tommie and I came around in the boat. She dived perfectly, then swam over to us to adjust some things, straighten out the towline, and get up the point of the single ski.

"Hit it!" she called. We took off in a blast of speed, and Dorothy emerged from the water, bending her body from side to side with the grace of a ballet dancer. We made an enormous circle as I watched Dorothy skim in and out of the wake streaming behind the boat. She made it look so

51

easy, but I knew it really wasn't. Then Dorothy and Tommie exchanged places, and Tommie was even better than Dorothy, if that was possible.

"Don't you want to try?" Dorothy asked from her place at the wheel. "Don't be scared. I remember my dad had to practically *force* me the first time. But I was only eight. He was such a great skier. He taught me everything. Once I got started, I loved it." She grinned encouragingly.

I shook my head, an odd feeling skittering through me. It wasn't that I was afraid I would look clumsy compared with these two. I knew, of course, that I would. It was something else—that same old clammy feeling that I got back home on Sunday mornings, when I wanted and I didn't want, both at the same time.

At lunchtime, I told Mother and Carson about my morning. They both looked pleased.

"That's wonderful, Angela," Mother said. I had always thought that Mother was very pretty, with her soft blond hair and slender figure, but now she just looked thin. The dark circles beneath her eyes worried me, too.

"They're trying to get me to ski," I added, "but I'm sure I can't. I'm not good at things like that."

"You could *try*, Angela," Carson said, "just the

way we're going to *try* to run this motel. We've never done anything like this before, either, so it's a challenge."

Sure, I thought. But why have all these challenges, when we could have stayed in Chicago, comfortably *un*challenged, among the people and things we knew best?

Carson went to the Chamber of Commerce that afternoon, then put up some posters in restaurants, and by that weekend, we had five units rented. I went water-skiing with the Ohlmsteads every morning under the blazing, relentless Florida sun. I learned that a skier should raise his arm when he surfaces after a fall, to signal the observer that he is all right. It was scary to see one of them fall but so reassuring to see an arm go up, straight and tall from the water, showing that the danger was over.

I stayed in the coolness of our apartment in the afternoons, reading or playing records. Sometimes, if I felt exceptionally lonely, I went over to the Ohlmsteads for a while.

Their house was furnished in cool-looking rattan, with straw rugs underfoot and strings of brightly colored beads hanging as a room divider between the tiny living room and the dining area. It wasn't like any house I had ever seen before, and it wasn't just the physical things that were different.

A spirit seemed to be in that house, a quality of love that moved among the family and knit them all together. It seemed to me the kind of love that only real families can have, not patchwork families like mine. Maribeth's family, back home, was like that. I remember once I talked to Maribeth about being able to *feel* love when it's in a house. Maribeth wrinkled her nose at me and said, "Oh, Angela, don't be silly."

Mr. and Mrs. Ohlmstead were as exuberant as their children and, like them, tall and slender and quick at everything. Mr. Ohlmstead joked that he had a real estate business with no customers. Mrs. Ohlmstead ran a private kindergarten. Dorothy and Tommie explained that they had wanted to work that summer but couldn't, because there weren't any jobs in such a small town.

In Chicago, I told them, there were all kinds of jobs. But Dorothy said that in Chicago, you couldn't live outdoors practically the year round, and they'd rather have fun and be broke.

And they did have fun. They cooked outdoors almost every evening, mostly hamburgers or chicken, and somebody always seemed to be stopping by for a visit or a swim. It was a place that, like a magnet, attracted everybody.

"Why won't you *try* to ski?" Dorothy asked one day when I was over there drinking iced tea. She was weaving paper mats for her mother's kindergarten class.

"You've been an observer long enough," Tommie added. "It's no fun just to *watch* all the time." He was lying on the floor, looking through one of his sports magazines.

"I couldn't start on one ski," I said. "That's too hard. Besides, I'd rather watch; really I would."

Shortly after that, Carson bought me a pair of skis. They looked very expensive, and I was sure he couldn't really afford them. Business was getting better, but not that much better.

"Now you don't have an excuse for not trying, Angela," Carson said. He looked at me thoughtfully, and his eyebrows went up a little. "It would mean a lot to me if you would."

We toured over to the boathouse the next day, and I couldn't have felt more scared. I couldn't get my feet in the rubber holders right. The points of the skis kept crossing, when they should have been straight. I felt like an ox. On the first two tries, I fell right off. On the next two, I couldn't straighten up, and my knees were about as flexible as two solid blocks of wood.

"You're just wasting gas," I called. I felt the tears in the back of my throat. I couldn't get the hang of it. Things weren't easy for me the way they were for Dorothy. Some people were just born with everything all in place, and others, like me, were splintered into a nobody.

"Just once more," Tommie called, circling the boat around again. "Don't give up yet. You've almost got it."

Swallowing hard, I tried again. I put everything else out of my mind, even all the instructions on how to ski. Suddenly I was up—really up—and hanging on so hard that I was sure my arms would wrench right out of my shoulders. But I was up!

Then, just as suddenly, I plunged off, deep, deep into the water. I flailed about frantically, fighting the water that surrounded me. Then I remembered that I had a life belt on. All I needed to do was relax, and I would be on the surface in a second. And I was. I raised my arm to signal that I was all right.

The boat circled around. It was harder to get my feet into the skis in deep water, but I managed finally to get adjusted.

"Hit it!" I called. Tommie blasted off, and I was up. It really was easy. I leaned back against the strain of the towrope and somehow stayed upright in the dead center of the wake. My hair felt as if it were going to fly off my head. But it was glorious, skimming over the water, light as air. Dorothy waved at me jubilantly as I gave her the thumbs up signal to go faster.

Mother and Carson were in bed that night, reading, when I wandered in to say good night. It used to make me feel uneasy, seeing them in bed. It was such a *married* place to be. But they *were* married, after all, and I'd got used to the idea.

"I got up on skis today," I said. "I'm glad you got me the kind you can single ski with, too. I'm going to try that later on, when I get better."

"I thought you might need that kind," Carson said, looking at me over his reading glasses and smiling.

"That's wonderful, Angela!" Mother said. She was suntanned by now, almost as dark as I was, and she had lost that tired, almost sick look. She seemed happier than I had seen her in a long time.

"I didn't think I could do it, but I did. It really was fun and not scary at all. Of course, Dorothy and Tommie helped. They made me believe I could do it."

"Sometimes people need help, but when you come right down to it, the doing is up to the person," Carson said.

I looked at him, suddenly thinking of what a chance he had taken, leaving his nice job to come down to this place, just to write a book. Carson wasn't happy-go-lucky like the Ohlmsteads. I knew he minded being broke.

A couple of weeks later, Dorothy, Tommie, and I packed a picnic lunch and stayed at the boathouse for a swim after skiing. We lay on the pier, full of egg salad sandwiches, bellies down, simmering in the noontime sun. I felt really pleased with myself, almost ready to try the single ski.

"Why don't your mom and dad ever go skiing?" I asked idly. It was hard to imagine this bright, happy group not doing everything together. They always seemed to.

"Oh, they don't enjoy it much, so we don't push them. Tommie and I have just as much fun alone," Dorothy replied.

I cupped my hand under my chin and gazed at the shimmering water. Of course Dorothy would take her family for granted. For a moment, I thought of Maribeth. It was the same with her. People surrounded with love don't understand how it is to have everything fall apart.

"But I thought you said your father taught you," I persisted.

"My real father taught me how to ski when I was little," Dorothy said. "My adoptive father was just never that interested in it."

I sat up, wondering if I had heard right. "Your *adoptive* father?"

"Yes. My parents died in an automobile accident a couple of years ago, and I was lucky enough to get a new family. The Ohlmsteads are really distant relatives—and Tommie got stuck with me as a sister." She rolled over and hit him playfully on the arm.

"But you're all so much the same! Like you're all cut from the same pattern. Not like us . . . like my family. None of us can seem to understand one another at all."

"Angela, you have some of the funniest ideas about families. Gosh, families are *people* before they're families. They all have their own—" She paused, as if searching for the right words, then added, "Maybe I just see it differently because I'm older than you are. Maybe I've seen more. . . ."

I lay back, shielding my eyes from the sun. The whole thing washed over me, back and forth like the tide. Dorothy, the one who really seemed to have it made, was an orphan. I imagined what it must have been like to lose everything in one horrible black moment, to feel cut adrift and alone. It must have been worse than the slow agony I'd had, trying to comprehend what had happened and where I fit in.

I thought about all these weeks that had flitted past—busy, new, wonderful weeks. I thought about how Sundays had come and gone just like any other days, except for going to church. There'd been no more clamminess, no more flutters of fear in my stomach, no more scenes like the one at Ned's graduation. There'd been only peace and sun and bright skies . . . and friends.

Looking back, I think I realized I'd been skirting around the edge of something deep and terrible, like an abyss with walls that could never be climbed. But I'd got around it somehow. I'd had a lot of help, of course, but *I* was the one who had safely reached the other side. I felt as I did that first time I fell off the skis—panicky at first, but then able to surface and raise my arm, to signal my friends that I was all right.

I knew then that I could go back to Chicago for Christmas and not feel so torn up inside. I thought probably my father had needed some time to heal, too, and that now we could both stop pretending. And then I wondered about Carson's sudden decision to write a book.

I went into Mother and Carson's room that night before going to bed. They were reading, as usual, Mother a novel and Carson his stacks of papers. I sat on the edge of the bed.

"Carson, I think it was a good idea that you had about coming down here." I looked at him cautiously. "Did you think I was going to have a terrible breakdown or something?"

Carson put his papers aside. "Not really. But we were worried about you. We agreed to get you away for a while, and I had always wanted to write this book, so we just put the two together. We thought we would go someplace completely different and see what happened." His eyebrows went up as he gazed at me over his reading glasses. "This certainly was different, and things *did* happen."

Mother leaned over to hug me, her eyes happy but suspiciously moist. Carson got extra busy with his papers. Suddenly I had a feeling that he had known about the Ohlmsteads all along. Oh, not about the adoption, perhaps, but just about *them* —that they would be so conveniently next door, that they would be so happy and friendly, that my summer would be so far from lonely.

But that was just a feeling I had . . . and with Carson, you can never be sure.

Boys Are
Like Algebra

Audrey DeBruhl

EXCEPT FOR BINKA, the whole thing never would
have happened the way it did—plus this big thing
I had about getting a date with Stuart Hamilton.
You know, it's really great to believe you can be
master of your fate, but now I'm beginning to believe a lot of important events in your life are just
a simple matter of timing. Binka's timing was definitely not good.

First, I should explain that Binka is a cat—not
just an ordinary cat, either. She's as black as coal,
with huge, green, intelligent eyes, and she has an
astonishing tail that crooks like a magnetized wire
whenever she gets upset about something. She is
terribly aloof with everyone but me, but then,

Binka and I have been through a lot together.

Also, you don't, at critical times, just ignore a pet that's special, simply because the most exciting and interesting boy in school doesn't seem to care much about cats. Maybe a Betty Jean Townsend does, but I do *not*.

Anyway, to get back to Stuart, I met him at an August beach party. It was an unbelievably dull affair—the sort of beach party that takes place endlessly throughout a Florida summer—with the same old faces making the same old remarks and everybody complaining that there was nothing to do. We were all sort of marking time, waiting for our senior year to begin and speculating on who would be new at school in the fall.

It seemed that every year, dozens of cute new girls and only a few nondescript, boring boys would turn up. It was hard enough at Jackson High to get a date with anyone interesting, without this influx of competition all the time. It simply wasn't fair. The school was small enough that we knew too much about everyone, like when they got the braces off their teeth, or fumbled the basketball and lost the big game, or warbled off-key at the Christmas concert. In short, we all knew everything unexciting about one another, and it seemed, at that particular point, that nothing very romantic was ever going to happen.

Then I saw this boy standing near the bonfire we had built to ward off the gnats. That's one of the things about Florida beaches in late summer. Gnats. Anyway, I saw this boy, a tall boy, with longish dark hair that curled in front of his ears and pointed in a V down the back of his neck. He was talking with a couple of other boys, and when he turned, I could see that he had huge, luminous eyes surrounded with thick lashes. His full mouth was curved in an uncertain smile. The firelight danced over him, flickering in a way that set him apart, as if he were the lead in a magnificent play that was about to begin. Everybody else seemed just part of the scenery.

"Who is that?" I whispered to Betty Jean Townsend, who was sitting next to me, squaw fashion, doodling in the sand. Betty Jean's father owned the drugstore, and she usually could be counted on to know everything that was happening.

"His name is Stuart Hamilton. Just moved to town a few days ago." Betty Jean glanced at him and then back at me. "You might be interested to know that I have a date with him tomorrow night." She got up slowly and brushed the sand from her blue bikini. Betty Jean has an absolutely super figure and loves to show it off anytime she can. She sauntered over to Stuart and smiled at him, rather possessively, I thought, for only knowing him a couple of days. I looked around for George Bennett, who had promised to bring me a Coke. George is a boy I date sometimes.

School started, and, of course, Stuart Hamilton wasn't in any of my classes. He was never in the halls or at lunch or at any of the places you usually see people. Finally I checked with the office to find out if he really was enrolled. He was. Then I figured he must belong to some club I could join. You see, I have this theory that boys are like algebra: They may seem very complicated, but all you have to do is find the common denominator, some interest you can share, and then just see what happens from there. I guessed Stuart must not have thought it was too great to belong to clubs, because he hadn't joined any.

Well, it was frustrating, to say the least, but the only one who knew about my big passion was Binka, and I could count on her not to say anything. That's one of the neatest things about animals and a big advantage they have over people.

Anyway, I'm the type who thinks girls should be people and not just decorate the background all the time, so I was busy getting the new Ecology Club organized and trying to shape up the cheerleaders, because I'm the captain, and drafting a change in the dress code to present to the student council. I still hadn't seen anything of Stuart Hamilton, but then came the day of the first pep rally.

I was yelling in front of the senior section, trying to get them to outdo the juniors, when I spotted Stuart. He was sitting off to the side, with a blue spirit ribbon pinned to his shirt. He looked as if he were trying to get with the whole thing but didn't know how. Our school really yells a lot, and I just knew he'd been to a school more sophisticated than Jackson and probably thought we were all being silly.

Everyone charged out when the rally was over, and I was outside pulling off my letter sweater, when I saw Stuart strolling out with Betty Jean.

"Hi!" I said, still feeling very exuberant, the way I always do after cheering. "Don't you think this was the best spirit ever?"

"It was okay," said Betty Jean languidly. "Stu, this is Connie Parks. She's probably the most *active* girl in school." The way she said "active," it could have been a synonym for *horrible*.

"Hello," I said. My voice sounded kind of strangled, probably because, from nowhere, a great, beating lump had just popped into my throat. Stuart Hamilton looked just as fascinating as he had that night in the firelight.

"I guess everyone knows Connie," he said. Stuart had a way of smiling that made my knees feel disconnected.

"I hope you'll like it here. It's a sort of small school, but we have a lot of fun."

"Oh, I like it, and now I think I'm going to like it even more." His gaze locked with mine, and I thought he had the most beautiful eyes in the whole world. They were . . . well, poetic is what they were. And I just knew, with the same clarity I had felt at the beach party, that Stuart Hamilton was going to ask me for a date, and not just an ordinary date, either. It would be something big and special, and we'd have a marvelous time.

We laughed and chatted all the way to Stuart's car, which was an ancient MG that looked very jaunty, and I thought it was exactly the kind of car that someone like Stuart Hamilton should have. But I had to go back to the girls' shower room and change for Ecology Club, so I just smiled and

69

waved good-bye—casually, I hoped—and walked away, wondering how I'd look in that MG.

Days upon endless days went by, and the phone rang constantly, but it was never Stuart. I was thinking that maybe I shouldn't have got into quite so many things. One evening I was lying on my bed with Binka, scratching her ears and telling her how I couldn't even *see* Stuart, much less find my common denominator with him, when I noticed something different about her. I stroked the thick black fur on her back, so she wouldn't get alarmed, and started rubbing her belly. She seemed to be getting very plump for such a slender cat. At first I could hardly believe it, but, of course, I knew. Binka was going to have kittens.

Weeks dragged by, and the Homecoming Dance was coming up. I was working on a design for the senior class float and was the decorations chairman for the dance, but I didn't have a date. I wasn't too worried, because George Bennett usually came through and asked me to things. Still, I did have this faint hope that Stuart would call. He had taken out just about everyone else in the senior class, and I thought that, sooner or later, he would get around to me. But waiting was sheer agony.

Then a couple of things happened. George asked Betty Jean to the dance, and that made me feel kind of funny, because I had always thought I could count on old George if nothing better came along. And then, at the last minute, Stuart called.

I had been very busy working on the float the evening before the dance, and I was kind of tired from punching paper napkins into the chicken wire that held our float together. Our theme was "World Peace," which was a pretty big theme to try to condense into one object. We built a globe with a dove on top, and, believe me, that isn't easy to create with chicken wire, especially when you're discouraged about not having a date.

"Hello, Connie?" It was Stuart's voice on the line. "Don't you ever stay home?"

"Sure. Sometimes. But I've been so busy getting ready for Homecoming. . . ."

"How about going to the dance with me? I know it's kind of late to ask, but I've been trying to get you for weeks."

"You have?" I was delirious with joy, of course, and the excitement carried me all through the next day while I worked on the decorations in the gym. At last the moment came for Stuart to appear, and I was just introducing him to my parents in the

71

living room, when I heard the most awful yowl from the kitchen. It was just one long, horrible sound, high-pitched and full of anguish.

"Oh, dear," my mother said, "I think Binka is having her kittens!"

I rushed to the place we had prepared for her, in the corner next to the dryer. Sure enough—a small black replica of Binka was already in the process of being cleaned up.

"We have to leave, Connie." Mother had followed me into the kitchen. "The Bennetts are expecting us for bridge, and we can't disappoint them."

I looked at Stuart, and I could see he was anxious to leave. I looked at Binka, and she stared solemnly back at me, her tail crooked like a broken antenna. Of course, I knew that cats have kittens all the time and don't particularly need any help. But I had so looked forward to the big arrival, and now I felt like a traitor for leaving her alone.

"We'll be home early," I said, forgetting all about the party we'd been invited to after the dance. "I'm sure everything will be all right."

Stuart opened the door of the MG, and I smiled brightly as I thought, *Well, this is my big date with Stuart Hamilton that I've been looking forward to for so long.* He'd have thought I was absolutely stupid if I'd told him I should stay home because my cat was having kittens.

We arrived at the dance, and everyone was milling around and laughing, but Stuart seemed very quiet. I just felt depressed. The decorations, which had seemed so beautiful that afternoon, looked limp and ragged. I didn't remember the gym ever being so hot or the noise so loud or my heart so heavy.

Stuart was a really great dancer, but he didn't dance much like the other boys at school. Also, it was getting to be a strain to keep thinking up witty and interesting things to talk about, so it was almost a relief when George cut in. Then I danced with a few other boys, and then I danced with Stuart again. The whole time, I kept seeing Binka and her crooked tail and wondering if something might be going wrong.

Finally I couldn't stand it any longer. Was I a real person or not? Could I pretend I didn't care that my cat was having kittens, just to please someone else? Why, Binka meant more to me than most *people* I knew, and she had a lot more character and loyalty, too.

"Stuart," I said, taking a deep breath, "I know

you're going to think I'm silly, but I just have to go home and see how Binka is. You can stay at the dance; that's okay. Just let me borrow your car, and I'll be back in a few minutes."

"It's okay, Connie. I'll take you home. I'm really not too crazy about dances, anyway." He smiled at me, but I wasn't too sure that he really meant it. Boys usually aren't very interested in cats.

I was unlocking the front door when I heard another of those awful yowls. We dashed in, to find that Binka had just delivered her fourth kitten and was tidily cleaning it up.

"Do you think she's all right?" I asked. I must admit I felt kind of ridiculous, now that we were actually back home—especially when I remembered that you can't get back into a dance once you leave.

"I think she's doing just fine. I used to live on a farm, you know, and I've seen lots of animals being born."

"You lived on a farm?" Stuart Hamilton living on a farm just didn't fit in with my picture of him.

"Sure I did. It was up in North Dakota, and we had everything—cows, sheep, pigs, the works." He leaned against the kitchen counter and shoved his hands into his pockets. "It's so different here, I

guess I'm having a hard time trying to fit in."

I stroked Binka gently and rubbed her ear in the way she likes. This was a whole new dimension of Stuart Hamilton, and I couldn't get used to the idea that my dream man was really a farm boy with problems. "Why did you move down here?" I asked.

"For my dad's health. His doctor thought we should move to someplace warm, so we sold out and here we are. But it's hard to move anywhere for your senior year . . . you know . . . not knowing anybody. . . ." His eyes looked wistful.

I realized that Stuart had told me more about himself in the last couple of minutes than he had all evening. Maybe it was because I'd stopped trying to impress him with how clever I was and had got around to asking him about himself.

"I didn't think you were the type to care so much about an old cat," he continued. "You always seem like such a rah-rah superstudent . . . not much like the girls I used to know."

I glanced up and saw that he was dead serious. "Don't you like girls who *do* things?"

I was getting kind of annoyed, because there it was again—that attitude that you have to be what people think you should be, that you have to stay in the background and be sweet and quiet, just because you're a girl.

"Sure I like girls who do things. But it seems to me that you do *everything*. Like you think the whole school would fall apart if you got sick and stayed home for a week."

I laughed. It probably did seem that way to a boy like Stuart, who probably thought girls should just bake cookies or something. And then I thought a little longer. Maybe I seemed that way to everybody else, too. It was just possible that I had gone a bit overboard trying to show everyone what a big individual I was.

"I think you've got a real point there, Stuart. But the dance is still going on, and the gym is still standing, and I'm here with you. Let's put on some records. We have a speaker in the kitchen, so we can listen in here."

While I was hunting for my favorite album, I realized something else. I'd been doing to everybody the exact thing I thought they'd been trying to do to me. To George, the dependable. To Betty Jean, the boy-crazy. I'd been making pigeonholes in my mind, where I could neatly place everyone, instead of trying to know them as they really are. I'd been so busy trying to show them all that I'm not just another girl but a *person,* that I was going to have to start all over again to get acquainted.

I hadn't dreamed that Stuart Hamilton had come from a farm in North Dakota. He just had to be glamorous because *I* had decided he was. I hadn't taken the trouble to find out that he was a very nice boy who felt a little lost and was having his own hard time finding a common denominator.

"Stuart," I said, coming back into the kitchen, "would you help me pick out some records—some that you like? We can put them on the stereo while we're waiting for the next kitten, if there's going to be one."

"I think there's going to be one." He was sitting on the floor next to Binka and her little brood, and I thought this sure was a peculiar way to celebrate Homecoming. Stuart looked up at me in a special sort of way, relaxed and peaceful, and happier than he'd looked since coming to Jackson. He smiled that nice slow smile of his, and for a beautiful moment, our thoughts sort of connected. It was as if each of us knew the other was happy and we were glad to be together and that was the only thing that was important. All the untrue things we had thought about each other just melted away.

I sat on the floor and touched his hand. I had

never felt so full of contentment, and at least I had been right about one thing: When boys seem too difficult to understand, all you have to do is find the common denominator. Boys really *are* just like algebra. Right?

Promise Not to Tell

Mary Knowles

MARTHA HAD JUST stepped out of the shower and into her bedroom, a terry cloth robe wrapped about her, when there was a sharp *ping!* against the window.

She started, then looked toward the Bascomb house next door. Cheryl was leaning out the window, her long, golden hair partly covering her face. Under the circumstances, the whole scene looked like the fairy story "Rapunzel." Martha tried to imagine that she could even hear a witch crying, "Rapunzel, Rapunzel, let down thy hair."

Cheryl motioned toward the blackboard she held. Martha went to get her own blackboard, wondering idly how many walnuts Cheryl had thrown against the window since she had been grounded the previous week and how many pieces of chalk they had used between them.

Cheryl wrote on her blackboard. *Meet me at Miller's Pond at 5.*

Martha wrote, *Going to dentist.*

Cheryl erased furiously, then wrote, *This is URGENT!!!!*

From the expression on Cheryl's face and the stubborn set of her jaw, Martha knew she wasn't kidding. She wrote, *I'll be there.*

Aunt Pearl came out of the Bascombs' back door then, and Martha thought she looked a lot like a witch, with her dark hair pulled straight back from her face and twisted into a bun at the nape of her neck. Her nose looked pointed and pinched and long. She had changed much in the six months since Uncle David's death from a heart attack.

As Martha erased the words from the blackboard, she thought about Cheryl's predicament. The week before, Cheryl had gone to the Holgate High Spring Fling with Rory Clarkson. On a sudden impulse, they had left an hour before the dance ended to drive up to Haley's Canyon for a hamburger and a Coke.

On the way back, the car had run out of gas, and

they'd had to walk the rest of the way. What with the heel coming off Cheryl's shoe, they hadn't got home until three in the morning. By then, Aunt Pearl—she wasn't really Martha's aunt, but the Bascombs and the Scovilles had lived side by side for fifteen years and regarded one another as practically "family"—was having hysterics, and Martha's mom and dad were over at Aunt Pearl's house, and Aunt Pearl had called the police.

Mothers were sure hard to understand sometimes. All the time hospitals were being called and the police were asking questions, Aunt Pearl was sobbing, "Oh, my baby! Why don't you find my beautiful little girl?"

But when Cheryl walked into the house, safe and sound, Aunt Pearl screamed, "How dare you frighten me like this? You are not going to leave this house for one solid month!"

"But, Mom, let me explain. Rory's car—"

"You'll explain nothing. Go to your room. And, Rory, get out of this house. I never want to see you again!" And then she slapped Cheryl's face, in front of everyone.

With her shoes still in her hand, Cheryl ran upstairs, tears streaming down her face.

Of course, Aunt Pearl had to reduce the sentence, because Cheryl's piano recital was Sunday night, in the Gold Room at the Hotel Alpine, and forty people were invited. Then on Monday, spring vacation would be over, and Cheryl would have to go to school so that she'd graduate from Holgate High in June.

But she hadn't been out of the house for a full week, and Aunt Pearl had guarded the phone like a dragon, so her only communication with Martha had been by blackboard.

Now Martha wondered, as she wriggled into her green and white striped dress, what could be so "URGENT!!!!" Maybe. . . . Since her father's death, Cheryl had come to loathe playing the piano, because her mother made her practice three hours a day. Maybe she had decided to break her hand or something.

Anyway, she'd go to the dentist early, and perhaps there'd be a cancellation. As she stepped into the hallway, she saw her sister, Diana, in her room at the end of the hall. She was wearing her white wedding dress, and Minnie Slade was on her knees, yardstick in hand, measuring the hem. Martha couldn't see Diana's face, but her mother was sitting in the pink satin slipper chair, looking up at Diana, and her face was radiant.

Mom had looked that way ever since the night Diana and Lance became engaged. Of course, Lance Fisher was a successful lawyer and the most beautiful man Martha had ever seen, and it was all pretty wonderful, because Diana was twenty-nine years old and had been crying every time she went to a wedding.

And then, bingo! She'd met Lance, and that was that. They were getting married next Wednesday, and everyone's life was suddenly charged with excitement—gifts arriving and being unwrapped, and people coming and going, and Mom and Dad and Diana and Lance and his parents off to parties almost nightly, all dressed up and smiling.

"I'm going to the dentist now, Mom," Martha called.

"Yes, dear, that's nice. Have a good time."

Martha was sure that she could have said, "I'm shooting myself, Mom," and her mother still would have answered dreamily, "Yes, dear, that's nice. Have a good time."

There *was* a cancellation at the dentist's, so Martha was finished in good time. She hurried home and changed for her meeting with Cheryl. As she pedaled out of the yard, she heard Cheryl playing a Brahms piano concerto. It sounded really great. Perhaps she was a musical genius, as Uncle David always used to say. Martha hesitated. Maybe Cheryl couldn't get away, after all. Well, she'd bike over to Miller's Pond and wait, anyway.

Cheryl was already there, sitting on the flat rock in the shade of the elm trees, gazing across the pond. "Cheryl! You're here . . . but . . . I heard you practicing and—"

"That's Van Cliburn on the stereo." Cheryl looked up, her eyes very blue and very determined. "Mom's gone to the beauty parlor to get her hair done."

"She has?" It was the first time she'd had her hair done since Uncle David died.

"Tomorrow night is the recital, remember? Her *big moment!* Agnes is there cleaning; Mom left her as watchdog. I told Agnes I was going to practice, and I shut the door to the music room and put on Cliburn. I sneaked out the side door. You know how Agnes is."

Agnes had a one-track mind. Piano music was coming from the music room, so Cheryl was practicing, period.

Martha sank down beside Cheryl on the flat rock. "And so what's so urgent?"

"First, you've got to promise me you won't tell . . .

anyone." Cheryl looked serious, and Martha remembered Mary Ann Thorn. Once they had been a threesome, but Mary Ann had repeated something Cheryl had told her in confidence, and that had been the end of Mary Ann, as far as Cheryl was concerned. A promise was sacred. In all their years as best friends, Martha and Cheryl had never broken a promise to each other.

"Yes, I promise."

"Raise your right hand."

Gosh, this must be really serious. Martha raised her hand.

"Your solemn, sacred word."

"My solemn, sacred word." A shiver went up Martha's spine.

"Rory and I are eloping tonight."

"Eloping? You've got to be kidding! You aren't even finished with high school yet!"

"We're not going to graduate."

"But Rory is going to be an engineer, and you and I are going to college next fall. We're going to be roommates!"

"Not anymore." Suddenly Cheryl began to cry. "Rory's parents are sending him to New York to stay with his grandmother as soon as he graduates. They're all determined to break us up! And you don't know what this week has been like, with Mom on my back every minute, making me practice three hours a day. *Three hours.* My fingers are ready to drop off. And I haven't been able to talk to anyone, not even you. But every night, after midnight, when I was sure Mom was asleep, I've called Rory."

"But, gosh, Cheryl, you shouldn't—"

"I love him, Martha—so much that if they separate us, I'll just die."

Cheryl looked ready to die. She'd lost weight, and her face was colorless.

"But how will you live? I mean, you have to eat and things like that."

"Rory can get a job in a lumber camp in Oregon."

"Oregon? That's about a million miles away."

"We're going to drive. Rory's been working on his car all week. I've got twenty dollars from my birthday money, and Rory has fifty dollars he earned working at the gas station."

"Oh, Cheryl, please don't go." Martha began to cry.

"Don't say that, Martha. We've *got* to get married—*now.*"

"You mean—" Martha sucked in her breath.

"Oh, not *that.* I mean, Rory really loves me,

Martha. We just want to get married and have each other forever, and if we don't elope, we'll never see each other again, and you've got to help!"

"How?"

"We need your dad's big ladder so I can climb out my bedroom window. Mom would hear me if I opened a door. Rory's coming at exactly midnight. You'll have to be quiet, or your mom—"

"They won't be home until after two. They're going to a dinner party for Lance and Diana in Jackson City."

"Good! Look, here's the route we'll follow." With a sharp stick, Cheryl drew a map on the flat rock. "By tomorrow night, we'll be over the state line, in this little town. See it? Curtis. There's no waiting period or blood tests or anything, and I'm *almost* eighteen, and Rory looks *twenty-one*."

It was true. Rory was tall and dark, with a mature-seeming intensity about him; he could easily pass for twenty-one.

Cheryl jumped up. "I've got to hurry back. Mom might get home early."

Martha stood up, too, and, all at once, the magnitude of what Cheryl had told her swept over her. "But we were going to have a double wedding after we graduated from college!" Her voice was a thin wail of bitter disappointment.

"I know! But this is the way it's got to be. I can't *talk* to Mom anymore. She's changed so since Daddy died, and I miss Daddy, and everything is all wrong." She bent her head and sobbed. "She slapped me, in front of everyone. I wanted to die right then and there. Maybe now she'll be sorry."

Martha's arms went around her friend. "I'll have the garage open, and I'll help Rory with the ladder," she said reassuringly.

Cheryl brushed the tears away. "Remember, you promised not to tell anyone."

"Don't get so uptight!" Martha felt a bit angry. "I promised, didn't I?"

Cheryl was gone then, and Martha sank down on the rock again, looking at the road map Cheryl had drawn, picturing Cheryl and Rory speeding along the highway in the red VW.

When she reached home, Mom and Diana were in the living room, knee-deep in tissue paper; gift wrap, string, and ribbon were being thrown every which way. Lance was leaning against the staircase, his pipe in hand, looking tall and masculine. Mom and Diana squealed in unison. "A blue casserole! It's beautiful!"

Lance laughed. "Anyone would think it was the

89

first casserole instead of the fifth." But he smiled, and his eyes sparkled.

Martha thought about Cheryl and Rory. There wouldn't be a nice, big wedding for them, and they wouldn't have even one casserole.

"Is something wrong, Martha?"

"Wrong?" Her voice squeaked. She looked up into Lance's eyes. They were gray and so piercing that Martha felt suddenly as if he were reading her mind. She had a sudden sympathy for any witness he cross-examined. "What makes you think something is wrong?"

"Oh— Let's go to the kitchen and have a Coke."

"Thanks, Lance, not now. I've got a paper to write for English. School starts again Monday, and, as usual, I've left everything until the last minute." She wanted to turn and run upstairs, but she forced herself to walk slowly.

Just as the family was leaving for Jackson City, Aunt Pearl came over. She looked pretty with her new hair-do, and there was a glow about her that made her seem younger. "May I borrow your lace tablecloth and silver candlesticks for tomorrow, Clara?"

"Yes, of course. I'll get them."

For a moment, Aunt Pearl stood there holding

the tablecloth and the candlesticks. "I decided, in a weak moment, to have Saunders do the catering. Forty people. That's too many for me to bake for." She sounded happy. "David wanted the recital to be very special, and I'm determined to have everything perfect."

Except that there won't even be a recital, Martha thought a bit wildly.

"You're coming, aren't you, Martha?"

So the ban was really being lifted! "You mean Cheryl and I can actually speak to each other again?"

Aunt Pearl's mouth tightened. "Someday Cheryl will thank me for what I did. She and Rory were seeing far too much of each other."

"You were very rude," Martha's mother said after Aunt Pearl had gone.

"Oh, Mom, I couldn't help it. She's been on Cheryl's back ever since Uncle David died. Before that, she couldn't have cared less whether Cheryl practiced or not."

"But, honey, can't you see that's why she's pushed this recital and why she has been so against Cheryl's getting serious with Rory? David had his heart set on Cheryl's becoming a concert pianist. And for some reason, he disliked Rory. Pearl used to *like* Rory. After all, he does come from a good family, and he's a nice boy. But since David died, Pearl probably feels guilty about liking Rory and not being enthusiastic about Cheryl's music, so she's determined that everything be carried out just as David wanted it."

"But she's treated Cheryl like a two-year-old."

"Yes, I think she's overdone it. I've felt sorry for Cheryl."

"Maybe someday Aunt Pearl will be sorry, too."

"What do you mean?"

Martha looked away. She never could lie to Mom. "I—I mean, maybe someday she'll realize that Cheryl misses her father, too, and I mean, well—" She stopped and just shrugged her shoulders, because Lance was watching her, and this time he wasn't smiling.

She went to her room, and after they all had gone, she went downstairs slowly, her heart beating dully. She felt sneaky and all churned up about what she was going to do. But she had promised Cheryl!

Dad had pulled the garage door down before he left. Now, with a heavy sigh, Martha lifted it. It was metal and made a horrible clatter, one Aunt Pearl would be sure to hear, even in her sleep, if

Martha opened the door later on.

Just before midnight, she sat on a bench on the patio and looked up at Cheryl's room. It was dark, but the moonlight was very bright, and she thought of the lines from *Romeo and Juliet:*

". . . by yonder blessed moon I swear,
      That tips with silver all these fruit-tree tops. . . ."

She waited, and still there was no light in Cheryl's room. *Maybe she's fallen asleep and there won't even be an elopement,* she thought hopefully.

A hand grasped her shoulder, and she gave a little scream.

"Ssh! For gosh sakes," Rory whispered.

"You scared me, you big lunkhead."

"Sorry. Let's get the ladder. Here, hold my flashlight." Did she just imagine that his voice cracked, as if it were just changing? In the moonlight, he looked tall and too skinny, as if he had grown so fast that he hadn't had time to fill out yet.

She held the flashlight while Rory lifted the long ladder off its hooks. Then he placed it against the house, under Cheryl's window, and still there was no light in the bedroom.

"Why doesn't she hurry?" His voice was frantic, and it *did* crack. He was a silly, skinny boy, and suddenly she hated Rory with a passion for taking away her dearest friend. She hoped that Cheryl was sleeping . . . would sleep until morning. But at that moment, there was a small squeak, and Cheryl was coming down the ladder, in pants and a jacket, with a small overnight bag in her hand.

Then she was on firm ground and in Rory's arms. For a long moment, they just clung to each other, and Martha felt awkward and in the way. She wondered if she should clear her throat, to remind them that she was there.

Finally Rory said, "Come on. We've got to hurry. My car is parked down the street."

They turned to go. "Cheryl!" Cheryl noticed Martha then. "Here's my pearl necklace and my blue scarf. Something borrowed, something blue. Remember?"

"Oh, Martha, thanks. Oh, gosh, Martha. I don't know—" She stopped, uncertainty in her voice, as if she, too, realized that what she was doing was sneaky and shabby and all wrong.

"Come on, Cheryl!" Rory whispered hoarsely. She gave Martha a last hug, and then the two were running out of the backyard.

For a full minute, Martha looked in the direction they had gone, then turned and looked up at

Cheryl's room. The ladder! The big oaf hadn't put it back! Struggling, she got it down and into the garage, scraping her leg in the process.

She went to bed, but sleep came slowly. Her scraped leg smarted and throbbed. Finally she slept, only to dream of a ladder that kept bending out of shape.

She was awakened by voices, Mom's, Dad's, Lance's—Lance had slept in the guest room—and, loudest of all, Aunt Pearl's.

Martha put on her robe and went slowly downstairs. They were all in the living room, clustered around Aunt Pearl, who was still in her blue robe. "She's gone! I found this note on her pillow. 'When you read this, I will be miles away. Please don't try to find me. Please just let me live my own life and be happy.' "

Aunt Pearl was crying, and Martha's heart softened toward her—until Aunt Pearl sobbed, "What will I do? The recital's tonight!"

Oh, my, yes! That blasted recital! That was all Aunt Pearl cared about! Mom looked up then and saw her. "Martha, do you know anything about this? Did Cheryl tell you she was going to run away?"

Martha stood there, her face hot, her throat

tight. How could she possibly answer?

"I asked you a question, Martha."

"Aunt Pearl hasn't allowed us even to talk on the telephone, remember?" The words came out fast. *That isn't a lie,* she thought. *It's an evasion.* But she saw the way Lance was watching her. She went into the kitchen, poured a glass of orange juice, and took a sip, but it tasted bitter, and she poured the rest down the sink. She heard a telephone call to Rory's parents. Yes, Rory was gone, too. She heard Aunt Pearl say, "Oh, Clara, my baby has eloped!"

Forever after, Martha was to remember that Sunday. Lance and Diana left for a brunch, and Aunt Pearl went home. Martha could see into the Bascombs' living room through their picture window. She watched Aunt Pearl pace the floor, still in her blue robe, saw her start every time the phone rang. After a while, Rory's parents came, and then the three of them paced the room. Rory's father gestured a great deal with his hands.

When I promised, I didn't know it would be like this, she kept thinking. Then she heard her mother telephoning to people, telling them the recital had been called off. And all the while, Martha sat stiffly on the edge of the big chair by the window.

It was three o'clock when Aunt Pearl came over. She was still wearing the blue robe, and her eyes were swollen from crying. "Oh, Clara, this whole tragedy is all my fault. I wanted to carry out the plans David made, and somehow I lost Cheryl while I was doing it."

She looked so old and kind of shrunken and pathetic. Martha knew that if she didn't leave the house, she might shout out the whole miserable story. She slipped quietly out the back door. Again she pedaled to Miller's Pond, and again she sat on the flat rock. She studied the route Cheryl had drawn. There, right under the ladybug, was Curtis, where Cheryl and Rory would be that night.

A twig snapped, and Martha's hand spread out, covering the map. Without a word, Lance sat down beside her.

"How did you know where I was?" Martha asked nervously.

"Deduction. Everyone has a special place he goes when he wants to think out a problem. For me it was the attic. I solved more problems sitting in an old swivel chair, with my feet on the windowsill. Martha, look at me."

She looked up at his face, but she could not quite meet his searching gray eyes. "Did Cheryl tell you she was eloping? And don't evade by saying, 'We weren't allowed to talk to each other, remember?' "

So he had known it was an evasion. She looked away.

"She made you promise not to tell, and a promise is a sacred thing, never to be broken. Am I right?"

She felt close to Lance, and she knew he would understand, but still she could not speak.

"Have you ever stopped to think that Cheryl wants to be found, before it's too late?"

"You've got to be out of your mind!"

"No, I'm not. Oh, she doesn't *know* she wants to be found. But think for a moment. Why did she leave a note, and why"—he gently lifted her hand off the route scratched on the rock—"did she explain so carefully where she would be, and when?"

"She doesn't want to be found! She and Rory are crazy about each other."

"There is nothing as intense as love at seventeen." He laughed wryly. "I know. I eloped, too, when I was seventeen."

"*You* did?"

"You've got to believe it. Her name was Susan. She had deep brown eyes, and I wrote poetry to her. And one night we eloped because our parents refused to let us see each other."

"You mean you've been married before?"

"No, thank heavens. Five miles from home, my car threw a rod. By the time we got home—the folks never did know we ran away—we were hungry and tired, and Susan was crying, and I had a blister on my heel. We never spoke to each other again." He whistled softly. "Was that a narrow escape!"

"And you wouldn't be marrying Diana next Wednesday." Martha's heart sank at the thought.

"Remember, Rory has college ahead of him before he can support a wife. And, Martha, think of this: A boy and girl should not get married because they want to get even with someone. It never works out. I sincerely hope Rory's car throws a rod before it's too late."

"Oh, Lance, if I told, Cheryl would never speak to me again."

"She would—someday."

"You don't know Cheryl. She's a real strong hater."

Lance stood up. "The decision rests with you."

He left, and Martha felt the special loneliness of having to judge right and wrong. For long, agonizing minutes, she sat there looking out over the pond, and she hurt as if she were being torn apart inside. The thought of betraying a friend. . . .

Then she remembered Cheryl and Rory sneaking away in the dark, and she knew the whole thing was very wrong.

Once she made up her mind, she realized that not telling was quite as wrong as all the rest of it. Still, it was hard to speak up.

"All the time Aunt Pearl has been going through agony, you've known all this, and you didn't even open your mouth!" Mom's eyes flashed.

"I couldn't just break my promise to Cheryl without thinking about it first. Could I?"

"Of course you couldn't, honey." Aunt Pearl's arms were around her, and she was once more sweet and understanding, as she had always been before Uncle David died.

Then the feverish activity began. A call to Rory's parents . . . plane reservations to make . . . and then Aunt Pearl went home to dress.

Martha didn't know she was crying until Lance said, "Don't cry, sweetie. You were brave to do the right thing. I know what it cost you to do it, too."

She stood up, then walked slowly upstairs. In the privacy of her room, she threw herself on the bed and sobbed, and when there were no more tears left, she sat by the window to watch and to wait.

Lance had said Cheryl would forgive her—someday. Her spirits lifted. Why, that someday could even be tomorrow!

Signals

Betty Ren Wright

SOMETIMES, when she walked the six blocks between the high school and her house, Carrie would
tell herself, "By the time I get home, I'll have a
plan." They were interesting blocks for someone
who expected to make a career of helping people,
though their attraction might not be obvious if you
drove past them quickly. The houses were small,
and they looked as if they had all been built by the
same contractor, with three styles to choose from.
There were a lot of open fields between the houses,
and in the distance was the grade school her twin
brothers attended, collapsed like a low heap of
blocks across a hillside. What was interesting about
the neighborhood was the way the houses took on

identity as people moved in, discovered what it was like to live there, and, gradually, displayed signs and signals that said, "This is what's happening." It seemed to Carrie that if she looked long enough and saw clearly enough, there would be revealed a truth, clean and inarguable, that she could take home and put to work.

Some of the signs were real ones—FOR SALE, perhaps, after just six months, and still no draperies at the windows. Or a HELPING HAND sign in a window, a fluorescent-painted palm that meant if a child was frightened by another child or by a creep in a car, he could run up to the door and get help. Some of the signals were more subtle—gardens that said, "Look! Enjoy!" and others that said, "Heaven help a weed that shows its face around here!"

The people-signals were the most interesting. Over there was a man cutting his grass, cutting too close to the geraniums and clipping off a couple of beauties. "Blasted flowers—if she spent more time cleaning the house and less time digging in the dirt, maybe I could find a place to sit down at night." Across the street there was an air conditioner going full strength, although the temperature outside was in the sixties. Somebody trying to drown out a fight? And there was a woman at a window, staring out, a dustcloth in her hand, not looking at a thing, just staring. "I didn't know it would be like this. I can't even remember how I thought it would be."

It was ridiculous to be so understanding about other people's problems and so fuzzy-headed about her own. Carrie reviewed the absolutes the way she had been taught in school: Given, parents who no longer seemed to like each other much. Given, seven-year-old twin brothers who didn't care about anything so long as they could make plenty of noise and have a lot to eat. Given, a house that was a long way from being paid for and greedily ate up money for repairs. Given, everyone getting crabbier and sadder and everything going down-hill. What she needed—must have—was a plan. All around her, strangers were signaling, and she could read the signals and sympathize. Why should she have so much trouble figuring out what to do in her own house?

A screen door burst open and a little girl ran out, with a woman right behind her. The woman had a rolled-up newspaper in her hand and was swatting wildly at her little girl's blue-jeaned bottom. Carrie turned her head. Coolness, she thought, that was the thing. Perhaps all it would take would be one person keeping cool, no matter what. If her father was snappish and sullen when he came home, she could stay out of his way and see that the boys did, too. If her mother was crying in her bedroom, Carrie could go and talk to her and gently tease her out of her depression. Maybe that was the way—to see it all and be untouched, cool.

There was another possibility. She could come on so strong that everyone else would have to forget their own problems and listen to hers.

"I loathe school—I've decided to drop out and get a job." No one would believe that.

"I have a terrible headache, like something pressing on my brain." Not bad, except that it would be impossible to fool Dr. De Mark for very long. Too, those tests would be expensive.

"I was attacked in the washroom." Effective, certainly, but her mother would want a detailed description of what happened, and her father would kill somebody. And there would be Dr. De Mark again. Actually, she was better suited to playing it cool.

Her favorite plan involved getting her parents to sit down with her and talk about their problems. That was a step better than keeping cool, since it meant that she would be actually helping. Years ago, when she was no older than the twins, her parents had talked together a lot. She could remember the murmur of voices in the living room after she went to bed, the wry comments over the morning paper, the telephone conversations, the planning of vacations.

Somewhere along the way, the quantity of words had lessened and the decibel count had risen. It had to do with her father wanting more money—wanting to change his life-style, whatever that meant. And it had to do with the twins, who, at seven, made her mother look waifish and unsure every time they charged into the room. It had to do with the new wrinkles her mother managed to discover in the mirror every other morning, and with her father's new clothes, and with the leak in the garage roof. Silly things, nothing much by themselves. The important thing was to consider them carefully and one at a time, to find logical solutions and then act, to choose a plan. As Carrie walked through the fields and down the freshly laid sidewalks, the sound of her mother's crying sometimes seemed to reach out to her from an impossible distance. *Nothing could ever make me cry like that*, she thought proudly. *Nothing and no one in the world.*

She was thinking about that—about keeping cool and objective and serene—that evening when she met the dog. He was the biggest dog she had ever seen, and he looked at her sullenly, his head up, his tail hanging limp. They met in the middle of a field; it was foggy twilight, and she didn't even see him until he growled. Though she was startled by the unexpected sound, she wasn't frightened at first. She liked dogs. But her quick "Hi, boy" was met with a snarl, and she saw that there was no chance of friendship here. He was full of hate. He had a dog's lifetime of hate spilling over in his eyes and in the way his ears went back. She started moving away, very slowly, saying things like "Good boy," and "Get the heck out of here," and "What a nice dog!" in the most soothing voice she could manage. The dog moved, too, tied to her with invisible threads of anger.

It occurred to her that if the neighborhood watched her with half the intensity with which she watched the neighborhood, someone would surely realize she was in trouble. Walking backward through a field ought to suggest that something peculiar was happening, even if the tall grass hid the dog from sight. But no one came or even called. They were all safe behind ruffled curtains,

cuddling their children or washing the dishes while the candles on the dinner table burned down. Or fighting, or changing fuses, or sewing patches, or doing anything but looking outside into the darkness.

"Say," she quavered, "let's be friends, huh?" It sounded silly when she said it, and the dog must have thought so, too, for she thought she saw his powerful hindquarters gather into the beginnings of a leap. Then her foot touched sidewalk—the wilderness of the field was past, and at almost the same moment, a car came down the street. She saw the lights approaching and moved quickly into the gutter, an arm raised to signal, while the dog hesitated. The car stopped beside her.

The door swung open against her back. "Carrie, get in!" It was her father's voice.

She whirled around into the car and pulled the door shut behind her, expecting to hear the crash of the dog's body against the metal. But there was only the idling of the motor and then her father's arm around her, pulling her close. Against all her principles, she began to cry.

"He was going to—" She looked out the window and saw the dog watching them, his eyes already glazing over with indifference, now that she was out of reach. "He wanted to kill me. . . ."

Her father gunned the motor. "Some fool is going to be out a good watchdog," he said. "I'll call the police, and they'll take care of him." He patted her shoulder. "Hey, you're really scared. I thought you *liked* dogs."

"I like dogs that like me," she said. It was too late for dignity, but she straightened up without moving away from his arm. "Do you have to call the police?"

He snorted impatiently. "How would you like it if some five-year-old tried to pet him?" he asked. "Use your head, sweetie."

He was being nice. She felt suddenly tired, like a baby in the cozy cradle of the car.

"I'll take you home," he said, and they were around the corner and halfway down the street before it occurred to her that it was an odd thing for someone who lived in the same house to say.

She turned and looked into the backseat. It was full of cardboard cartons and a couple of suitcases. She recognized her father's typewriter case and saw his golf clubs on the floor. His plaid cap—his picnic hat, they used to call it—was on top of one of the boxes.

He pulled up in front of the house. "That's the

picture, love," her father said. "I'm leaving. I can't take any more fighting; neither can your mother. We've agreed that this is best all around." He waited, but she was thinking about the times when he used to wear the cap, and she didn't say anything. "You'll understand when you're older. The boys will, too." He waited again. "Anyway, I'm not leaving town. We'll see each other a lot. It'll really be easier, you'll see."

She kissed him good-bye and went up the walk, reading the signals as she went. The draperies in her parents' bedroom were drawn; her mother would be in there, crying. The television set was on full blast in the living room, and there was a light in the kitchen. The boys were almost certainly going through the refrigerator, eating everything in sight. The evening paper would still be neatly folded on the hall table, where her father always liked to find it, unopened.

She was right on all counts. She separated the boys, pale and uneasy tonight but still loud, and heated a can of chili for their supper. She soaked a cloth in cool water and went in to her mother, who was lying with her face to the wall and did not speak or even blink when the coolness touched her forehead. She turned down the television and straightened up the living room and washed the supper dishes. At eight thirty, she ordered the boys to bed, and she did ten algebra problems and read eighteen pages in her history text before going to bed herself.

At twelve she was still wide-awake. She walked quietly around the house, pausing at her mother's door until she heard a soft snore, then peeking in at the boys, who lay like rag dolls flung across their beds.

She was cool, objective, serene. Most of all, she was relieved. That was a surprise, because she had always assumed that a plan of action had to be imposed from outside, like a uniform you chose to wear, unrelated to your real feelings.

Back in her own room, she stood at the window and looked out at the other houses. Most of them were dark, but there was one lighted window with a shadow moving across it occasionally—maybe a mother taking care of a sick child?

Unexpectedly, she remembered the dog. He was out there, too, prowling through the dark and the fog, nursing his anger for perhaps the last time. Hurriedly she went to the kitchen, filled a dish with some meat scraps, and put it outside the door, just in case.

"Take care of yourself," she whispered into the blackness of the yard. "Keep cool."

When she went back to bed, she cried a little, very softly, because the dog was so alone, and after that she was able to go to sleep.

Daddy Is
a Little Doll

Constance Kwolek

DADDY TALKS to himself.

One afternoon last summer, I decided that I
should cultivate an odd habit of my own. Should
cultivate? *Must.* I decided this while sulking over
a can of ginger ale in my bedroom studio.

"There isn't a thing wrong," I told myself, "with
a seventeen-year-old girl practicing voodoo, as
long as it's for a good cause. Nothing destructive—
just a little white magic to make everyone's life a
lot happier. As pastimes go, it's no more bizarre
than some others I can think of."

Not that Daddy's is an odd habit entirely. His
solo dialogues, unlike mine, tend to be profitable.
He is an author in the mystery-and-murder field, a

prolific third after Georges Simenon and John D. MacDonald. It is a vocational necessity for him to carry on conversations while alone in his den, where he does his writing.

Besides, Perry Flanders, Sr., is not himself when he talks to himself. He is Detective Inspector Descharmes and any one of a number of suspects, accomplices, and perpetrators.

Last year, he suddenly began addressing me in the same accusatory tones used by his fictitious detective inspector.

"Where were you on the night of April seventh?" he'd ask me, twirling his horn-rimmed glasses by one bow, his blue eyes boring down into mine. This scene invariably occurred in the entrance foyer, just after I had arrived home.

"April seventh is tonight, Daddy. Roger and I went to a movie, and you know it."

"A likely story," he would say, pacing with deliberation before his lineup of one female suspect.

"It's time for our midnight snack." I'd divert him hastily, heading for the kitchen. "You set out the cups and saucers, and I'll make our cocoa."

"Pairing off" was all he really suspected me of, and he was right—up to a point. I was an accomplice in only a negligible amount of amorousness, a perpetrator of only the custom of dating. When it involved his only child, however, my father considered that custom a felony.

"I have my own plans for my own future!" I muttered rebelliously in my room that summer afternoon. My father had just sabotaged a water-skiing lesson with a boy named Morris. "And I have plans for you, Daddy dear," I added ominously.

Perry Flanders, Sr., is by no means a villain to me. Daddy and I love each other dearly—a bit too dearly, it began to seem to me.

Who had poured at all the literary teas given him by ladies' groups since she was thirteen? Who had always been a gracious hostess at publishers' parties? Who had been his housekeeper, cocoa maker, and typist? Miss Flavia Flanders, that's who!—devoted daughter of the "literary giant," as my equally devoted father's press releases call him. Over the years, I had lulled myself into a false sense of servility upon which my father had become much too dependent.

"And it has to stop!" I told myself, clearing my worktable of its remnants and tape measures, its needles and pincushions.

It wasn't just by whim that I had costumed the

117

cast of the senior class play. I planned to continue as an artist and designer, in addition to becoming, eventually, the wife of some nice man—if my father would ever become romantically involved with some other potential housekeeper, cocoa maker, and typist for long enough to let go of me.

I got down to business, unmindful of the strands of hair sticking to my damp forehead and my perspiring neck. Not a single wistful thought of Lake George intruded on my intentions.

First, I made a Daddy doll.

He was a jaunty character with quizzical eyebrows and slender limbs. Using swatches of fabric, I outfitted him in a T-shirt and tennis shorts similar to those my father was actually wearing during that afternoon's den-pacing debate. The doll was becoming a fairly faithful likeness of Perry Flanders, Sr.

"Nothing from *The Exorcist* or *Rosemary's Baby* for you," I murmured to it/him as I worked. "This is not the traditional fiendish incantation coming up—merely a mild enchantment. After all, you are a person very dear to me. I am entirely justified.

"Justification," I added to myself, "is the fact that I am a brotherless child."

I was just beginning to toddle, and Daddy was

a novice writer, when my mother died. At that time, Perry Flanders had had nothing published under his now-famous name.

"So it wasn't a matter of your being stuck with your original by-line," I told the doll. "Print is so— so irretrievable! Why did you keep adding 'Senior' to your name? Obviously, you've always planned on a 'Junior' in your life."

Next, I made a wife doll for Daddy.

No taller than he and sparingly rounded out with foam rubber (for I well knew my father's thoughts concerning genuineness in individuals, especially in women), she was a lithe and perky companion for the Daddy doll I had made.

"I'll let your face go, for the moment," I told it/ her gently, after I had sewn her into a simple dress of a neutral shade. Then: "Remember, this is only pseudo voodoo. . . ."

I cleared all pins away from the two of them. Next, with painstaking stitches, I embroidered their hands together with a tiny heart of red floss.

Their clasped hands, silent companionship, and obvious affinity delighted me, for the pair seemed to exclude all others—particularly a daughter/ stepdaughter who had her own life to live.

The face of the lady was a problem. How might

I conjure up intelligence, warmth, and humor with a few dabs of acrylic? I was holding my breath over a rendering of her pink smile, when the doorbell chimed.

"Darn!" I said. Her mouth had smeared. I was dabbing at it with a dampened paint rag, when the chimes sounded a second time.

"I'll get it," I called out as I went down the hall to the front door. There was no stirring from Daddy's den—only deep murmurings as he conscientiously questioned and answered himself.

"Good afternoon!" The lady chirped on cue when I opened the front door. "Cosmetics time again."

"We don't want any," I said automatically. Then I got a good look at her. I shut the door and stood with my back against it, gasping. *What had I done?*

"Skin freshener?" she called from the porch. This was the lady who came to our door several times a year. Now, still mesmerized with horror, I listened to her recitation as it zeroed in on her real reason for visiting our house. "Moisturizer? Bath oil? Cologne? Ah—men's cologne? After-shave for Daddy?"

I gulped, turned, and flung the door wide.

"Why don't you try us again in . . . in six months?

And besides, ma'am—" Slowly, I brought my eyes up from her walking shoes to her trim beige suit and carrying case to her impeccably made-up face —that is, impeccably except for— "May I say, ma'am, that you are not a very good advertisement for your products?"

Her blue-lidded eyes widened.

"Your . . . your lipstick is smeared," I forced myself to tell her, my voice reduced to a raspy whisper. When I shut the door, gently this time, she was searching frantically in her carrying case, probably for a mirror. As her hurried footsteps faded, I ran back to my room.

Coincidence—that's all it was!

"I'm sorry. I'm sorry!" I babbled to no one as I scrubbed at the face of the wife doll on my worktable. *Start from scratch,* I told myself. *The natural look, a girl who likes walks in the country, with the sun and the wind on her bare face— Uh-oh!*

The sound of the doorbell halted my confusion. With growing apprehension, I went to the door.

A complete stranger stood on the porch—a youngish pioneer-mother type, *clean-scrubbed face innocent of makeup,* solid and amiable in her faded but crisp cotton dress. Her eyes shone with a fond twinkle as she spoke.

"I have reason to believe that you could use a housekeeper in this poor motherless home," she began. A fan of my father's? Yet— Her faintly accented speech immediately evoked, for me, visions of scrubbed corners, lemony oiled furniture, and succulent stews followed by richly fruited and nutted desserts.

"My references are magnificent. And none of my employers minded the songs, Miss Flanders."

"The songs?" I echoed.

"The little ditties I compose."

A fan? An opportunist! What I had interpreted as fondness had turned out to be pure avarice, unmistakable in the glitter of the eyes in that *soap-and-water-clean* face!

"You wouldn't believe it, dearie," she went on— and on. "Piracy, it is. Some of the songs you hear every day, on every Top Forty radio station—those are *my* songs, *stolen* from me. I am sure that himself knows all the right people, and he could help me. All I need is someone to pull a few strings. I'm a real gifted songwriter, you know—"

"We already have a housekeeper, thank you," I interrupted, pulling myself up to my greatest height. "Her name is Flavia Flanders." I shut the door firmly.

Flavia Flanders had had her fill of witchcraft—or so it seemed at the time. In my studio room once again, I found it difficult to determine whether my project bored or frightened me. When I had half-heartedly painted a passable new face on the wife doll, I gave her one last look before I abandoned the entire scheme. Her eyes were a trifle too widely spaced, although her smile was engaging enough. . . .

Chilled all over again by the two encounters on our doorstep (Coincidence. Sheer, unadulterated coincidence—the smeared lipstick, and then the scrubbed, fresh face on the alleged songwriter), I suddenly wanted the dolls out of my sight. I set the hand-holding twosome on top of a cupboard, wedged beneath old term papers of mine and several of Daddy's first drafts, precious only to me. I found out later that this was the worst—or the best—possible place to have secreted the romantic pair.

"Stale, absolutely stale," Daddy told me over our light summer dinner that evening.

"The croutons? The eggs?" I asked, surprised. My Caesar salads and mushroom omelets invariably drew raves from him.

"No. Me. The new book." He drained his glass of minted iced tea. "My work has gone completely cold. I feel as though I'm chipping at a block of granite instead of writing. What I need is a new outlook. Flavia, have you ever felt that the two of us are vegetating?"

"Vegetating?" I forced my face to seem open and innocent. *You're on the right track, Daddy dear. Why don't you get out of the house so that I can get out of the house—with Philip or Roger or Morris, one of whom will be telephoning me any minute.*

"I've been arguing with myself all afternoon." His eyebrows were more active than ever, one creeping into the artistically long hair fringing his forehead, the other frowning behind his glasses. "No offense, dear, but I'm tired of your company as well as of my own."

"Then why don't you walk around the block, talk to the neighbors, get out of yourself for a bit?" I suggested nonchalantly, running the water for dishes.

But he puttered around, going into his den to sharpen pencils and riffle through manuscript pages. The clock was inching nearer to the time for a phone call from a boy, and I was growing

125

increasingly nervous as the minutes ticked away.

At last he made his jaunty way down the hall to the front door, twirling his tobacco pouch by its rawhide drawstring. He was just in time to answer the door.

I was so engrossed in kitchen chores that I never heard any conversation. When I went to the front of the house to sit by the telephone, Daddy was still home—and he had a guest.

". . . and at the age of thirty-seven," she was telling my father in a melodious but matter-of-fact voice, "I feel it is long past time for me to graduate to writing adult fiction."

Her few words managed somehow to embody intelligence, warmth, and humor—and my thoughts flew to the wife doll sitting atop the cupboard in my bedroom.

Just then, Daddy saw me outside his den and invited me in to meet his guest. I took a closer look at the woman.

She wore a shirtwaist dress the color of wheat, about the color of her glossy hair. If her gray eyes hadn't been so widely spaced, she would have been stunning. Even at that, she was a very attractive woman. Thirty-seven? Hard to believe that she wasn't much younger than Daddy. I began to feel a strange excitement—and then I saw what she was holding.

In her hands, unmistakably, she was holding a manuscript.

Daddy hates amateur writers. Rather, he fears and dislikes them. We average one a week—someone with a poorly conceived (but unwritten) novel in him (more likely *her*), coming to our door to beg for the magic secrets that only Perry Flanders, Sr., can impart. His only secret is that he does hard labor at the typewriter, and no one wants to hear this.

We had already had our amateur for this week: the songwriting lady who had come to the door earlier. But—

"Tell me again, Christina. How many children's books have you had published?" Daddy asked her, as if he were reading my mind. She named a number of books that nearly matched his own output over the years.

"What typing service do you use?" I asked her, feeling my excitement returning. From where I stood, her manuscript seemed not to have any strikeovers. Such neatness is secret, magic, and very professional.

"I do all my own typing. I don't like to let my

work out of my sight, except when I mail it to my publisher," Christina said, smiling at me almost apologetically.

These were precisely the sentiments of Perry Flanders, Sr. He flashed me a smile, his eyes sparkling as they do only when he has in mind a new character or a brand-new plot—or, as in this case, a great new idea.

"Think I'll take your advice, honey," he told me. "A nice walk around the block, while Christina and I discuss her literary career. There's the phone. Why don't you answer it? I'm sure it must be one of your young men."

"See you later, Flavia." Christina put her arm through Daddy's. No taller than he, I noticed, and —sure enough!—lithe and perky.

Philip and I saw them later. We were dashing about the tennis courts at the park, when the two of them went strolling by beneath the white birches. They were much too deep in conversation to notice us.

The next day, during my water-skiing lesson with Morris at Lake George, I glimpsed Daddy and Christina on the excursion boat.

And, on a night when Roger and I got lawn tickets to a concert at the Saratoga Performing

Arts Center, Daddy took Christina to the film festival nearby.

All this was over a year ago. Since then, Daddy has broken through his block of granite. His newest book appeared in time for the Christmas gift season—and it was his new wife who hostessed at his publisher's party.

However, Christina Flanders has regressed in her own writing. Instead of the career girl series of books with which she was so successful, she now writes preschool texts. When Perry Flanders, Jr., is learning to read and to count, he'll have all kinds of materials to work with, right in our home. You see, Daddy finally has a son.

I baby-sit for my little brother, but only occasionally. I am usually much too busy with dates, Civic Theater costumes, and designs for the fabulous boutique I plan to have in the shopping mall.

I am also much too busy and much too old to play with dolls. I am not childish enough to favor superstition over pure coincidence!

My only project even slightly related to dolls is a clay mannequin that sits on a corner of my worktable. He is an Apollolike creature with a firm chin and tender eyes.

I haven't ever spoken a word to him.

Well, actually . . . you see, I'm not sure how to address him.

The fact is, I can't decide whether his name is Morris or Roger or Philip.

Second Best

Willie Mary Kistler

STANDING on the top step of the Mallory front porch, Ann looked down at her cousin Judy, who was curled up on the chaise, reading. Was she really as beautiful as people said? Ann wondered. It was difficult to judge someone you knew so well. Not only was Judy her cousin, but she was also her best friend, and they had lived next door to each other since they were children.

Ann tried to study Judy objectively, looking carefully at her pale, tumbled hair, her long, amber eyes. There were seven enchanting freckles across her nose—Ann counted them—like one quick sprinkle of cinnamon.

Ann sighed. Everything that had been said about

131

Judy was true. Was it any wonder that practically every boy in town, every boy that counted, anyway, hung around the Mallorys' house after school? The girls were there, too, of course, but only the "in" girls, those lucky enough to be Judy's friends.

A heady business for Judy—and for Aunt Margaret, who was so ambitious for Judy—this popularity thing that had happened to her. So it wasn't surprising, Ann told herself, that the Mallorys had changed so much.

"Wear your yellow voile tonight, dear," Mrs. Mallory called to Ann from a chair at the end of the porch.

Ann kicked restlessly at a pebble lying on the step. "I'd thought about my blue dress, Aunt Margaret."

Mrs. Mallory's brows drew together in a distressed frown. "But I'm sure the yellow would be best. Don't you think so, Judy? You in your cream shift and Ann in the yellow. The two of you will be perfect."

Perfect for what? Ann asked herself rebelliously. *You mean I'll be a perfect foil for Judy, setting her off. No, I'll wear the blue,* she thought. Then, seeing how genuinely troubled her aunt was, she decided wearily that there was no use in making

132

a fuss. If Aunt Margaret cared that much, what did it matter which dress she wore? This was so typical of her sweet, light-minded aunt, always thinking the wrong things were important. Still. . . .

"Wear the yellow," Judy said in her new, imperious way.

Because her face felt suddenly hot, Ann turned away. It was one thing to wear the dress to please her aunt but quite another to do it because Judy demanded it. *I'll wear what I like,* she thought fiercely, *and I'll tell Judy so.* But she didn't; the words blazed in her mind, but somehow they couldn't get said.

Finally Ann answered, "All right!" and ran blindly down the steps and across the yard. *It's not important,* she told herself over and over, trying to ward off the rush of shame that she always felt when she gave in to the Mallorys.

But giving in to Judy was a way of life for Ann these days. Walking slowly up her own driveway, she puzzled over the situation, not really understanding it herself. All she knew was that when she did try to stand up to Judy, she started remembering scenes from the past.

She remembered things like the time at Laguna Beach, when she and Judy were twelve. They'd

133

been caught in a riptide. Judy, much the better swimmer, had stayed as close as possible to Ann, calling to her in an even voice, steadying her. "Don't swim toward shore, and don't panic when you feel yourself being carried out to sea. We mustn't tire ourselves, and we must swim *across* the riptide." And then she had added, in an encouraging shout, "We'll make it!" And they had. They had reached the quiet water some distance out, but, unwearied, they were able to swim triumphantly back to shore.

She remembered the lovely smell of baking in the kitchen on rainy afternoons. Aunt Margaret, cooking for one of her numerous benefits or club meetings, would listen, absorbed, to all the school gossip and not say a word as Ann and Judy steadily ate a wide path through the cooling cookies.

Most of all, Ann remembered that for a long time after her mother's death, when she was eleven, she had felt compelled to flee the emptiness of her own house in the late afternoons and had run next door. She had found Aunt Margaret always there— Aunt Margaret, who had been so busy before.

They were still there, of course, both Judy and Aunt Margaret, anytime she needed them; but everything was changed now.

Two years ago the change had begun. That was when the new beauty and confidence had come to Judy, when Judy had found herself riding the crest of an almost incredible popularity. She was not just a popular girl but *the* most popular girl in senior high . . . vice-president of the student body . . . undisputed leader of the envied crowd.

But hadn't Judy carried Ann along on this wave of popularity? In second place, certainly, but how many girls would have given *anything* to change spots with her? And, forcing herself to be honest, she admitted that this was the second reason she couldn't hold out against Judy. Ann liked her coveted niche in the high school hierarchy—a niche that had its price, she thought, feeling the shame flare brightly again—and she didn't dare to risk losing her position by defying this new Judy, who had grown so demanding.

Ann ran up her own steps as though fleeing from someone. Reaching the front door, she slammed the screen behind her as she went inside.

Then, surprised to see her father at home and in his favorite chair across the room, she forced the disturbed look from her face and smiled at him. "I didn't know you'd be home early this afternoon, Dad."

Her father marked a place in his book as he closed it. "I sneaked off from the university. Don't report me to the authorities."

Ann's smile deepened into a grin. "Wouldn't think of it," she said.

Dad smiled back and then asked casually, "And how are things going with Judy and your Aunt Margaret?"

"About the same," Ann answered, just as casually, but she felt strangely humiliated. Dad was looking at her in an interested, speculative sort of way, almost as if he had guessed something of what had happened at the Mallorys' just now.

"Your Uncle George tells me that Judy didn't do at all well on her college boards," he persisted.

"No. I expect she hasn't studied as much as she should have—"

"I expect she hasn't. Not for a long time now," Dad replied, and, although he spoke easily, the words were charged with disapproval.

Dad thinks I don't see the change in the Mallorys, Ann thought miserably, *and he's trying to make me see. He hasn't guessed that I've known all along but haven't had the courage to break away.*

Caught in a fresh wave of humiliation, Ann,

hearing a sound in the kitchen, turned from her father in relief. "Who's that? I thought Mildred was away this afternoon."

"Bob Morgan came by. He's been here for quite a while, and I told him to fix himself a sandwich."

Ann felt herself getting the tightened-up feeling that always came now when she knew Bob was around—a senseless feeling, because it shouldn't matter to her whether Bob was in the kitchen or not. She hadn't known him for long enough to care that much. He was fairly new in school, and it had been in only the last month that he'd started coming by in the afternoons.

"Why didn't he come on over to Judy's house?"

"Couldn't say. I told him you were probably there, but he said he'd like to look over some science articles I wrote last year."

Ann wanted to race into the kitchen, but she forced herself into a careless walk. As she went, she wondered again why Bob never followed her over to Judy's. Most new boys would have wanted to get in on the fun, to be included in such a special crowd.

"Hi, Bob," Ann said.

Bob was leaning on the sink counter, and since he was taller than any of the other boys Ann knew, there seemed to be a good bit of him to lean. He was studying the science article intently. A half-eaten sandwich lay on the counter beside him.

"Hi, Ann," he answered, and his blue eyes darkened as they touched her.

"What's in that horrible sandwich?" Ann asked.

"Mayonnaise, pickles, peanut butter, ham, and cheese."

"Sure you're getting enough to eat?" Ann grinned.

Bob grinned back at her, and they both laughed. "Fix you one?" he asked cordially.

"No, thanks." She went to the refrigerator, and because Bob's eyes made her feel confused and warm, she took a long time pouring herself a glass of milk.

And then, somehow, she had to ask. "Why didn't you come on over to Judy's and join in?"

"Well, I really didn't think about it," Bob answered. "I was reading this article your father gave me."

Then Ann knew that she was going to ask another question. It had lain at the back of her mind, like a little unopened package, ever since that first afternoon when Bob had turned up at her front door. She remembered how surprised she'd been, although she'd seen Bob in math class, where he

138

sat two seats down from her. She'd been curious because he was new in school and she liked his looks—but that was all.

Then, late one afternoon, there he was, ringing her front doorbell and, odder still, looking as surprised to see her as she was to see him.

"Well, hello, Ann," he said. "I didn't know you lived here."

Ann laughed ruefully. That was a new twist!

"You're not Professor Hale's daughter, are you?"

"I certainly am. Shouldn't I be?"

Bob seemed to think this over for a minute. "It follows, I guess. Advanced math and all."

Bob explained that he'd read one of Professor Hale's books as an outside reference in a science course, and he wanted very much to meet her father, to ask him a few questions. He hoped it was all right to come barging by this way.

Ann asked him in to see her father, and she was amazed as she watched Dad and Bob talking together almost as contemporaries, as old friends; but as Bob began dropping by regularly, she found that she, too, felt as though she'd known him for a long time.

She discovered something else, too. When he came near her, the blood sang in her veins . . . a strange and exciting song.

What a silly thing, to feel that way about him! He'd never taken her out; she wasn't even sure why he came to the house.

And there she was, back at the question. "Do you come to see Dad or to see me?" Ann choked over the words, but she had to know.

There was a long pause, long enough for her to hear the wind stirring in the tangerine tree at the kitchen window.

"I came at first to see your father. But now— You know why I'm here," Bob answered quietly.

Ann reached out with shaky fingers and tightened the lid on the mayonnaise jar.

"Is that all right with you?"

"That's all right with me," she answered, and she let out a little sigh of joy, knowing that this was what she had been waiting to hear.

"I wasn't going to tell you how I feel about you, because I can't run around much, and a popular girl like you. . . ." He drove his hands into his pockets and looked away from her. "I have a job delivering for Johnson's Pharmacy on weekends, sometimes even in the evenings, and I study hard. I want a good choice of colleges when I go next fall, so grades are important."

"None of that matters," Ann said.

She smiled happily, and, without saying any more, she and Bob automatically began putting the food away. Mildred, the housekeeper, was only part-time, and since Ann pretty much ran the place in her time out of school, her friends helped pick up when they visited.

Now, with everything done, Bob and Ann turned and looked at each other.

"Shall I drop by this evening?"

"Yes," Ann replied. She felt as remote and radiant as a star. "There's a party at Judy's tonight," she added absently. "We'll go over, and I'll introduce you to everyone."

Ann thought she saw Bob's expression alter a little—or was it only a fleeting shadow cast by the tangerine tree?

He gave her a level look. "Whatever you say, but I'll have to pull out for an hour during the party. I told Mr. Johnson I'd spell him at the soda fountain around nine tonight. Maybe you'd like to come with me."

Ann hesitated. "I don't know whether Judy and Aunt Margaret would want me to leave. I'll see how it goes."

After Bob had gone, Ann shampooed her hair

and brushed it until it glistened. That evening, she hummed as she dressed, and she kept changing her lipstick, hunting for the perfect shade. Taking the blue dress out of the closet, she hesitated, her fingers tight on the hanger. After a moment, she carefully replaced the blue dress and took out the yellow voile; as she did it, she felt two spots of color come into her face, as though hot coins had been pressed against her cheeks.

But she had become expert at burying her shame, expert at pretending the shame wasn't even there. By the time she finished dressing and went down to the living room, she felt at peace again. She smiled at her father, who was settled in his chair once more, the inevitable book on his lap.

"Where to?" he asked, returning her smile.

"Just over to Judy's to a Coke party. Can't you hear the music?"

"So that's what that dreadful din is," Dad commented dryly.

Ann laughed, and then she added, for some reason glad that she could say this to her father, "Bob's taking me."

There was an odd little silence, and Dad glanced down at his book. "Bob's a pretty independent sort," he said carefully. "Are you sure he'll get on with Judy and Aunt Margaret?"

Ann once again had to brace herself against the impact of sudden, stinging humiliation. Dad had always considered her a pretty independent sort, too—until lately. Was he comparing her with Bob and finding the comparison disappointing?

"I'll be in early," she said quickly. She hurried out onto the porch and stood there waiting, twisting her fingers tightly together. Seeing Bob come up the walk, she rushed down the steps to meet him.

"Oh, hi, Ann," he said, surprised. "Where's the fire?"

"I just wanted to show you I could be on time." She laughed, but the laugh had a quiver in it.

"I didn't know good-looking girls were ever on time," he answered, and as they started off down the walk, he reached out and caught her hand; lost in new excitement, Ann forgot her troubling thoughts.

The party was already under way when they reached the Mallorys' patio. Everyone was dancing to a stereo in the gold, uneven light of the Tiki torches lined up around the patio. Aunt Margaret, settled on the garden chaise and glancing through a fashion magazine, looked up in surprise and smiled. Her eyes, curious, rested on Bob.

Judy, spotting Ann and Bob, moved out of the dancing and came over. "You're Bob Morgan, aren't you?" she asked, smiling her slow, beautiful smile.

"Bob dropped by and I brought him along—" Ann, suddenly breathless, bit her lip until it ached. She had never seen Judy look lovelier. "You know each other from school then." The words came out almost in a whisper.

"Same English class," Bob said.

"We're awfully glad you could come." Judy was watching Bob, and her eyes had turned golden in the flickering light.

"Nice of you to let Ann bring me," he answered politely, and then he glanced indifferently toward the dancers.

Seeing this, Ann felt relief surging through her; then she turned anxious on another count. Judy's face held cold surprise, and Ann thought uneasily, *Judy won't like this. She's not accustomed to indifference. And Bob won't get on with the others if he doesn't get on with Judy.*

Judy went off with Jim Mercer, and Ann took Bob's hand, saying, "Come and meet Aunt Margaret." Pulling him around the edge of the dancers, she brought him up in front of Mrs. Mallory.

Ann introduced them, and Aunt Margaret sent Bob her sweet smile, but Ann could almost hear her aunt's thoughts: *So this is the new boy. Now, I wonder about his family, just who they are. I'll have to ask Judy to find out about him.*

"Ann's spoken of you, Bob, and we're glad you could stop by. We like to know Ann's friends, because—" She hesitated, uncertain how to go on, and Judy, coming up beside them, finished the sentence for her.

"Because Ann belongs to us, you know."

Bob turned and looked at Judy directly. "Does she really, Judy?" His voice was still easy and polite, but there was a penetrating, adult sound to the words.

"Yes, she really does," Judy answered as she turned away.

Ann felt a thrill of dismay. *Bob* must *get on with the Mallorys, because*—and here she put her feelings about him into words for the first time—*he means so much to me. And if the Mallorys don't accept him, the rest of the crowd won't bother to get to know him.*

Someone had put a slow record on. Bob reached for her, and they danced off through the shadows, but Ann felt as though she danced through light. For a while, she hardly remembered the Mallorys at all.

After the dance, she took Bob around and introduced him, and as she spoke his name, she heard the words come out with a pride she had never felt before. She saw how easily Bob moved among her friends. A lovely warmth settled around her. With the warmth, the fast, noisy dancing, and the laughter, she lost all track of time.

She was startled when Bob said, "It's nearly nine, and I'll have to spell Mr. Johnson now. I'd better explain to Judy and make a run for it. Will you come?"

"Maybe I. . . ."

They went over to Judy, who was standing with a crowd around Aunt Margaret, and Bob explained what he had to do.

"You mean you're leaving the party so soon?" Judy sounded shocked.

"Just for an hour or so." Then he added, "This is something I promised to do." Turning to Ann, he asked again, "Want to come along?"

Ann hesitated, wishing that Bob had explained more fully, wishing that he had tried a little harder to get on with the Mallorys.

147

"I may need some help with the refreshments later on," Judy said quickly, looking at Ann.

Hearing the unmistakable coldness in Judy's voice, Ann answered reluctantly, "I'll just wait here, if you don't mind, Bob."

After Bob had gone, she felt a rush of loneliness. She was glad when Mike Fairfield spotted her and pulled her onto the dance floor.

Immediately, she was back again in the shining circle of her friends, comfortable and reassured. But she kept glancing at her watch, waiting. And because of her preoccupation, it was a while before she knew.

She didn't know how she knew; it was something felt rather than heard, and it sent a fierce, bright shock through her. The word was passing from person to person, as soft as a whisper of wind in the trees: "Bob Morgan won't do."

Ann, sickened with disbelief as she remembered how everyone had seemed to like Bob, looked across at Judy, who seemed to be explaining something to Aunt Margaret. The word had gone out from there, then, just as she had been afraid it might.

Judy's verdict: Thumbs down!

When the record ended, Ann excused herself to

go over and sit down next to Judy. Aunt Margaret seemed preoccupied with her magazine, but Judy turned to Ann and said easily, "Everyone's meeting here again tomorrow night, before the basketball game. Come early and eat with us."

No mention of Bob, Ann thought bitterly. "How do you like him . . . Bob?" she asked, lifting her chin a little.

"He's attractive," Judy said, letting her eyes slide away from Ann's face, "but I don't see why you think he's so great. And the way he just up and pulled away from the party. . . ."

"He promised Mr. Johnson," Ann said miserably, and her face felt white in the torchlight.

Aunt Margaret glanced unhappily at Ann. "Perhaps, Judy, if you gave Bob another chance, got to know him a little better—"

Judy shrugged. "Okay. If it'll make Ann happy. He's not the kind I'd choose for myself, but— Well, bring him by tomorrow night, anyway, Ann."

Not the kind she'd choose! Give him another chance!

The words rang like a harsh bell in Ann's brain, and the shame that she had hidden for so long broke out into the open at last; she knew that this shame she had accepted for herself she could never

149

accept for Bob—because *he* would never have accepted it.

And she realized, too, that the thing you can't always do for yourself you can sometimes do for someone else.

Seeing that Bob had returned and was crossing the room toward her, Ann got to her feet and turned to face Judy.

"You'll be here tomorrow night then?" Judy asked into a strained, waiting silence.

For an instant Ann hesitated, finding the first step out from the crowd a lonely one. Then, "No," she began unsteadily, and she held her eyes away from Aunt Margaret, because the remembering might come back, confusing her, and Ann knew what she had to do.

"I'm afraid Bob and I can't make it tomorrow night," she went on, and to her surprise, she found the second step out was an easy one. She smiled pleasantly at the Mallorys. "We have other plans."

Those Dorn Girls

Dorothy Dalton

TRISH DORN stood in the doorway of the kitchen, watching her older sister, Meg, add another item to her shopping list.

"Honestly," Trish said, "I don't know why you asked that creepy Sylvia to dinner, too." She slammed a cupboard door shut.

"I told you, Trish: Mrs. Creighton understood it that way. Anyway, what's one more for dinner?"

"If it's Sylvia," Trish hooted, "one too many!"

Meg fluttered about, checking the contents of the shelves against her list. Trish shook her head. She had never figured out why Meg wanted to become engaged to a zero like Rolf Creighton in the first place.

Not when that dreamy, blue-eyed, black-lashed hunk of masculinity, Mike Parrish, was casting longing glances in her direction. Only Meg just couldn't see Mike. Frankly, Trish thought, Meg saw the Creighton standard of living, which spelled security—something the three Dorn sisters had had to struggle for since the death of their parents five years before. But Rolf Creighton—really!

At that moment, a loud crash sounded from the basement. Meg and Trish looked at each other, then ran for the steps.

"Kix, are you all right?" Meg called.

Kix was Catherine, the youngest Dorn sister and an embryo scientist, who practically lived in the basement with twenty-four white mice (at last count) and four hamsters.

They heard cries of anguish from below as they descended. Kix was crawling around the basement, trying to capture furry little white mice. Two of them ran up the steps, and Trish gathered them up.

"Oh," Kix wailed, "why am I such a clumsy oaf?" She clutched mice and returned them to their cages as she spoke. "That's the second time this week that shelf has collapsed."

"Why don't you fix it properly?" suggested Meg quietly.

"Good idea. I will, as soon as I get a minute. Every time Mr. MacDonald, next door, drives into his driveway, the wall shakes and down comes the shelf . . . and down come the mice."

"Hickory, dickory, dock!" Trish laughed, crawling out from behind the furnace with another pair of mice. "There—how many more?"

"Let's see—twenty-two, twenty-three—one more."

Meg dusted off her hands and went upstairs. "You girls keep looking. I have to get to the store before it closes."

Kix scrambled among the jars and boxes and finally emerged, dusty and triumphant, with mouse number twenty-four. Outside, they could hear the barking of their shaggy dog, Pushkin. He had probably seen Meg getting into her car. He looked upon all their activities as his personal business.

Trish tapped on the window. Pushkin looked at her, then let up on the chain and sank down, a bundle of white fur.

"That dog."

"He's a dear," Kix said absentmindedly as she set the cages back on the still-insecure shelf. "Whew, what a mess. Well, that's the way it goes with us scientists." She went to wash her hands.

153

"What do you think about Meg and Rolf getting engaged?" asked Trish, watching the hamsters frisking about in their cages.

"I think Meg's dopey. Why does she want a saddo like Rolf, when she could have a neat husband like Mike?"

"Agreed."

"Meg's conservative, but that Rolf—he's really a chilly character."

"But loaded," Trish added.

"And working in his father's bank makes him a good risk." The girls went up the stairs together.

Trish said, "I wish Mike would look at me the way he looks at Meg."

"Mike's too old for you," said Kix. "You're only eighteen; he's twenty-five."

"He's twenty-four, and I'm going on nineteen," Trish argued hotly.

"Well, he can't see anyone but Meg." They went to the kitchen, where Kix started munching on a chocolate cookie.

Trish nodded. "Guess I'll have to settle for Jim."

"And I'm stuck with Biggie. But at least he's bright and lots of fun and a fellow scientist." Swallowing the last bite of the cookie, Kix peeled a banana. "Biggie has possibilities, . . . Mr. Barlow

Barnes—*Barlow!* Every time I think of Biggie harnessed with a name like Barlow, I could choke. His mother must have been frightened by a cognomen before he was born."

They chatted amiably for a while before going upstairs to do their homework. Trish was graduating from high school in June, and Kix was a sophomore. Meg had been working for four years, since her own graduation. Trish often wondered if Meg resented having to forgo college to help keep things going for the three of them. But she seemed to like the insurance office and had had several raises since she'd been there.

Trish's thoughts were still on Meg as she settled down with her history book. The engagement would be formally announced at the dinner tomorrow night. There would be seven in all—Mr. and Mrs. Creighton, Sylvia, Rolf, and the three Dorns.

Meg was an excellent cook. Everything would be as perfect as she could make it. But Trish wished Meg were not settling for the snooty Creightons. Mrs. Creighton was a clotheshorse type, very chic, and busy in all sorts of community affairs. Sylvia, who was in Trish's class, was a replica of her mother. She would be attending a fashionable school in the East in September. Sylvia set Trish's teeth on edge, and Trish ordinarily went out of her way to avoid meeting her.

The doorbell rang, and Trish called, "I'll go, Kix."

Mike Parrish stood in the doorway, in his hands a radio and under his arm a set of rabbit ears.

"Hi, Mike. Come on in." Trish spoke in honeyed tones.

"Hello, squirt. Where's your big sister?"

"Out."

"Well, I fixed the FM radio and brought the new TV antenna." He went over to the TV set and turned it on. Trish placed the radio on top of the bookcase.

"Where's Meg?"

"*Out*," she said emphatically.

"You said that. Out where?"

"If it's of vital concern, shopping. A special dinner is about to take place, which will leave one less Dorn girl available." Trish looked at Mike as she talked. He was so handsome. Why couldn't Meg see the love in his eyes? Maybe she did see it and chose to ignore it. Meg had a rather aloof quality about her, and her natural dignity made it almost impossible to discuss things like love and Mike with her.

156

"Engagement?" Mike asked. His face flushed, and he looked a little sad. "Meg and that Creighton drip," he said disgustedly.

"Yes," said Trish woefully. "Can't you do something, Mike?"

"Me?" Mike shook his head. "She can't see me for *gold* dust." He sounded angry.

"Meg's not like that!" Trish retorted.

"Yeah, sure. . . ."

"Well, she isn't. Maybe she's had to be a little conservative—things being the way they were—but Meg's a fine person, and she wouldn't be influenced by money alone. Rolf's not some kind of ogre, either."

"I tried to get my message across, Trish. Meg wasn't having any. At one time, I thought we might—" He sounded wistful. He tightened the last screw on the back of the TV, gathered his tools, and stood up.

"There are other Dorn girls," Trish ventured.

Mike chuckled. "Tigers," he said, ruffling her hair. He walked to the door just as Meg, struggling with bags of groceries, opened it.

"Allow me," Mike said. He took the heavy bags to the kitchen.

"He brought the radio," Trish explained.

"Good. We can have soft music in the background tomorrow night."

Trish snorted and walked upstairs very slowly, watching Mike as he returned from the kitchen and spoke to Meg.

"I hear you're getting engaged," he began.

Meg's face froze. "Yes."

"Well, lots of luck." The words sounded sarcastic. Trish lingered on the stairs.

"Thank you." Meg's tone was totally innocent of emotion.

"I did sort of have some hopes along those lines myself, you know," Mike said after a second's silence.

"Sorry, Mike."

"You always had that icy wall around you, Meg. But I wanted to keep trying to thaw you out." Mike's words were uttered lightly, but the undertone of truth in them came through to Trish's ears, if not to Meg's.

"Really, Mike," Meg protested. Trish knew she shouldn't be listening, but she couldn't tear herself away. She wanted Mike to tell Meg how much he loved her; everyone else knew it.

Mike took a step toward Meg, pulled her into his arms, and kissed her soundly. When he released

158

her, Meg turned on her heel and walked away from him without saying a word.

Mike looked at her retreating back for a few seconds before he opened the door and let himself out. A moment later, the truck roared out of the driveway.

"Wow!" said Trish under her breath. She decided to go downstairs and see how her sister was taking it.

Meg was sitting at the kitchen table, her head buried in her arms. She was crying softly.

"Meg, what is it?" Trish asked, not letting on that she had been a witness to the little scene.

"Trish?" Meg wiped her eyes quickly and turned to face her. "Oh—" She started to cry again.

"Something Mike said?" asked Trish.

"It's too hard to explain."

"Why not try?" Trish persisted, seating herself.

"I don't understand my feelings myself." Meg sniffed. "I like Mike an awful lot, but something inside me wants something different."

Trish was silent. Meg had never confided in her before. She knew that if Meg were not terribly upset, she would not be doing so now.

"And I do love Rolf. I admire him, too. He's efficient and conscientious. And Rolf is a very nice

159

person, Trish. You'll like him better when you really get to know him. He's not mean or stingy, and he's more mature than Mike could ever be."

Trish thought that Meg was protesting too much. All those qualities meant *dull* to her.

Meg continued, "And he's not snooty like his family. But I don't know—there's this feeling. . . ." Her voice trailed off, and she gazed, unseeingly, out the back door.

"I guess it can be a fat problem, choosing a husband," Trish reflected. "I'll probably make a few choices and then end up with Jim after all."

"What?"

"Nothing. I just said choosing was a problem."

"I've already chosen," Meg said determinedly, her defenses back in place. "It's raining. Let Pushkin in before he barks his brains out."

"What brains? That dog—really, you'd think he was made of spun sugar."

She got up and went outside to release the animal. Pushkin danced around like a demented thing, tangling Trish in the chain and causing some purple language to fall on his shaggy white head.

"Dumb dog," she muttered, getting him loose at last. He ran in front of her, nearly upsetting her. When she opened the door, he took a flying leap into the kitchen. Having greeted Meg as if after months of separation, he ran into the living room to roll on the maroon rug, leaving telltale white hairs everywhere.

"Basement!" Trish shouted, and Meg pointed. Pushkin looked hurt and slunk away. Trish closed the basement door after him.

"Much as I like the dog, it would be easier to keep house without him," Meg commented, looking at the hair-covered rug.

Some hours later, when the Dorn sisters had settled down for the night, Trish lay awake, wondering about Meg and Mike and Rolf and wishing she were getting Mike Parrish for a brother-in-law instead of Rolf Creighton.

The next afternoon, all three girls were on hand to get the house in order for the dinner party.

Meg turned on the FM radio. It sputtered and squawked and was silent.

"I thought Mike fixed it," Meg said dryly.

"He did. I'll call him. He can check it again and have it back before eight tonight," Trish said, rushing to the phone and dialing Mike before Meg could protest.

"All set for the festivities?" Mike asked when he came by at one-thirty.

"We are," Meg said shortly. Kix looked at her quizzically. *What's wrong with Meg?* her look said. Meg was rarely in bad humor.

Meg stalked off to the kitchen to check the cake, which was baking and sending its delicious aroma through the house.

"I'll have the radio back in time," Mike promised. As he left, he winked at Trish. Maybe, she thought, like a modern Lochinvar, Mike would ride up in his white truck and snatch Meg from Rolf's arms.

Dream on, girl, she told herself.

By six forty-five, the house was sparkling. Fresh flowers stood in vases. The furniture was waxed and gleaming. The low bowl on the dining room table had clusters of white and pale purple lilacs in it. Their perfume mingled with the smell of the roast, making each breath a delight.

"You used every dish and glass in the cupboard," Kix said ruefully. She had visions of doing dishes far into the night.

"I'll help clean up, Kix," Trish promised. "Anything is better than listening to Sylvia on her favorite subject: Sylvia."

"She must talk about other things."

"Yes—Sylvia's clothes." They giggled together.

Meg stood in the middle of the living room, looking about her. "Doesn't the house look nice?" She smiled. "Thanks for your help."

"Well, we want you to be living proof that good housekeepers come in pretty packages," Trish said.

"Yes," agreed Kix, "and what's good enough for the Dorns is good enough for the Creightons." Kix smirked. "What's her first name, anyway?"

"Amelia, and he's Roland."

"Suits them," said Trish.

"Well, I'm off to shower. Keep an eye on the roast and on that Pushkin character," Meg said.

"He's outside. And if it doesn't rain, he won't even make the scene. Meg, you have nothing to worry about," Kix assured her.

At seven fifteen, Mike rang the doorbell and handed Trish a small tape recorder.

"Listen, I couldn't get the bugs out of the radio. I have some tapes of soothing, ring-cinching music here." He came in and looked around. "Pretty—all ready for the slaughter."

"Mike!" reprimanded Trish.

"Sorry, but I'm less than joyful that the only gal I ever went totally mad over has chosen a fellow less worthy and more moneyed than I. I'm the bitter type." He grinned wryly.

Mike was honestly suffering. Oh, that Meg really needed a good shaking up! Couldn't she see Rolf wouldn't be one bit of fun to live with through the years? Mike was a charmer, full of energy, and one day he would have money, too. Meg evidently didn't care to wait.

"Here, Trish, plug the recorder in. You push here to start it and"—Mike pointed—"this button to stop it." He waved at the girls and left.

By ten to eight, the sisters were dressed and waiting. The meal was almost ready to be served. Promptly at eight, the doorbell rang. Meg went to the door.

Mr. and Mrs. Creighton said, "Good evening," and Sylvia looked down her nose and said, "Hello, Miss Dorn." Rolf was turned out in his usual impeccable taste: dark suit, white shirt, dark tie. His blond hair was carefully combed. He gave Meg a quick kiss on the cheek.

Trish watched the little episode. Looking at Meg's face as she closed the door behind the Creightons, Trish thought Meg looked as though she wanted to run off into the spring night and never return. It was just a fleeting expression, and a moment later, Meg looked perfectly composed once again.

Trish and Kix—Catherine, as the Creightons called her—took the women's coats. After Trish had hung Sylvia's in the closet, Sylvia brushed past her to straighten it a trifle.

"Hope you don't mind, Trish, but the coat is brand-new."

"Lovely," said Trish, in her best social manner. Strangling guests, after all, was a thing her family had always frowned upon. If Meg wanted these stuffed shirts, she was going to have them—even if Trish had to socialize herself half to death!

Meg suggested a predinner cocktail, and Mrs. Creighton said, "Well, of course, the men do have one. I never do. I consider alcohol bad for the skin and for the figure."

Drip! thought Trish. She went to the tape deck and switched it on. Immediately, soft, mellow music floated out. Mike had certainly chosen well.

Meg served the men cocktails, settling for a small glass of sherry for herself and Cokes for the girls. Mrs. Creighton refused the Coke as well.

The conversation glued itself to safe topics—the weather, school, Sylvia's spring wardrobe, and Rolf's recent success in landing a new account

165

of some substance. While Mrs. Creighton rambled on, bragging about Rolf's ability, he became very uncomfortable and sent Meg a look that was a call for help.

Meg and Trish excused themselves and went to serve the dinner. Trish brought in the baked potatoes, the spinach soufflé, and the hot rolls. Meg carried in the beautiful roast.

"Mr. Creighton, will you carve?"

"Margaret, I'd be delighted." He seated his wife, and Rolf saw to the rest of the girls. Conversation ceased as the food was passed around the table. The tension was so great that Trish felt its presence was a living thing.

When the meal was finished, they lingered uncomfortably over their coffee. Finally, Rolf cleared his throat loudly, breaking the silence, and said, "We all know why we are here, of course, but, to make it official—Meg has consented to be my wife." He smiled happily, and Meg returned his glowing look.

"We're very happy to welcome you to our family, Margaret," Mr. Creighton said.

"Yes, Margaret, very happy," echoed Mrs. Creighton, but her tone was much cooler.

"Wish you two lots of happiness," Sylvia added,

sending a small smile toward her brother.

"We hope you'll both be very happy, too," Trish said, feeling like a traitor to the cause.

Kix jumped up suddenly and said, "Excuse me, but it's nearly nine and I haven't fed my mice yet."

"Mice!" repeated Mrs. Creighton with a genteel shriek.

"White ones. I'm doing a study on nutrition." Kix hurried toward the basement.

With her attention drawn from the table, Meg suddenly became aware of the patter of rain. "Trish, please bring Pushkin in, before he gets frantic."

"That dog!" Trish sighed and sent her eyes toward the ceiling in exasperation. She explained Pushkin's aversion to rain to a totally disinterested audience. Pushkin's barks were becoming frenzied.

Mrs. Creighton turned to Meg. "I think it's very generous of you to keep a dog. They require such a great amount of care." Her nose rose an inch higher. "What breed of dog is this Pushkin?"

Meg chuckled. "He's a you-name-it—part sheep dog, part collie, and all shaggy."

"You mean you have no papers for the dog?"

"Not since he was a puppy," Meg replied facetiously. Fortunately, the remark was lost in the

167

fracas of getting Pushkin through the kitchen door on his chain. Pushkin bounded back and forth, barking gaily as he pulled toward the dining room and Trish edged him toward the basement.

"Good heavens!" said Mrs. Creighton. "He's huge!"

Sylvia and her mother exchanged glances. A definite chill fell over the party. Trish came back to her seat, a little out of breath. In the background, the music played softly, filling in the many awkward silences. Ironically, Mike was helping the situation.

Suddenly the music stopped. Mike's voice came through the speakers: "Testing, one, two, three, four. Meg, I love you. Testing, one, two, three, four. Meg, I love you. . . ." Meg's face flamed as she shot out of her seat and headed for the tape recorder, which kept repeating, "Meg, I love you. Testing, one. . . ."

At the same moment, Mr. MacDonald drove into the driveway next door, and a crash, followed by a shriek, came from the basement.

Rolf leaped to his feet and headed for the basement, with Trish at his heels.

"The mice—the mice—" shrilled Kix. "There they go—" As Rolf opened the door, white mice scurried past his feet into the kitchen.

"Are you hurt?" Rolf asked anxiously.

"Just my feelings." Kix looked up from her kneeling position. "Two of the hamsters are gone, too." Pushkin gamboled about, thinking it was all great sport. He barked and batted at the mice. He had been taught not to take them in his mouth, but a swipe from his paw could knock a mouse silly. He bounded around until he knocked a bottle of red poster paint from another shelf. The jar crashed to the floor, and most of the splashing paint landed on Pushkin's shaggy coat. Frightened, the dog ran around the basement, dripping red paint everywhere he went.

"Oh, Kix," said Trish forlornly, "tonight of all nights. It's a catastrophe."

Kix started to cry. Rolf patted her shoulder and hurried toward the steps. Kix and Trish followed Rolf. They could hear Mrs. Creighton screaming wildly—the mice had invaded the dining room.

Mrs. Creighton and Sylvia were standing on the dining room chairs, clutching their skirts. Mr. Creighton was wringing his hands helplessly and watching the two hamsters run about in a corner of the room.

Meg stood transfixed, listening while the tape

repeated, "Meg, I love you. . . ." She pushed the OFF button at last and turned to survey the wild scene in the dining room.

A hamster ran past her, and she managed to gather it up in one hand as she caught a white mouse in the other.

"Kix, get some cages!" she shouted. "Please, Mrs. Creighton—they won't hurt you." Rolf helped his mother down from the chair.

Trish thought that this was probably the worst thing that had ever happened to Meg. No nightmare could be as horrifying.

Pushkin, who had been bouncing around at Trish's side, caught sight of Mrs. Creighton and decided to introduce himself. He covered the dining room in one leap and threw himself bodily on the poor woman, wet paint, shaggy coat, and all. Mrs. Creighton was beyond protesting. She looked down at her new blue suit, now spattered with red paint.

"Roland," she said, her voice a hoarse whisper, "take me home."

Meg wished they would all go home. Perhaps someday, when the wounds were healed, she and Rolf might marry and then move far, far away.

Loudly, Rolf said, "You're all making too much

of this. The whole thing was a series of accidents. Catherine didn't plan it this way." He looked over at Meg. "The tape recording I'm not so sure about."

Meg blushed and said furiously, "That Mike Parrish—"

Mr. Creighton alternately wiped his brow and patted his wife's shoulder. "Amelia, simmer down. The dog was merely showing affection."

"Oh!" howled Mrs. Creighton. "Affection! Look at me!" Paint had dripped from her suit onto her stockings and shoes.

"It's only watercolor," said Kix helpfully. "It'll come out." Her doubtful look belied her reassuring words.

Suddenly Mr. Creighton started to laugh. His wife looked at him as though he had gone mad. He laughed all the harder, until Meg, Rolf, and even Kix joined in. Amelia and Sylvia refused to see any humor in the situation.

Kix caught the last mouse and went down to the basement. Rolf followed and helped Kix to recage the hamsters. They chained Pushkin to prevent further outbursts of affection.

When Kix and Rolf returned from the basement, the Creightons were gathering coats, preparing to make their exit. Their thank-yous were somewhat cool, which Trish thought was understandable. What an evening!

Rolf told Meg, "Listen, I'll be back—I want to talk to you."

Meg sighed. "Oh, Rolf, I don't know. It was such a miserable mess. . . ."

"Put it out of your mind for now. See you later," he said as he hurried after his family.

Exhausted, Meg slumped down on the sofa. Trish and Kix cleared dishes. On one of her trips to the dining room, Trish saw Meg absentmindedly switch on the tape recorder. "Meg, I love you. . . ." Trish grinned as Meg angrily snapped it off again.

"I'd like to give that Mike Parrish a piece of my mind right now," Meg said. She added, a bit more calmly, "I'm going to put on some slacks; then I'll come and help."

After the dishes had been done, Kix went broodingly to her room. Trish had tried to cheer her up, but she couldn't be shaken from her low mood. Meg was tidying the kitchen, and Trish went out to the porch for a breath of air.

The night was moist from the recent rain and sweetly scented. Trish took a deep breath, feeling the tension ebb a little. Suddenly a figure appeared

173

out of the dark, walking slowly across the lawn.

"Hi, Trish," a male voice said.

"Mike?"

He came up on the porch and sat beside her.

"Meg is hopping mad at you."

Mike looked at her, all innocence.

"You and your tape."

"Well, I thought I'd get the message across once and for all—give her something to think about before she got herself hooked to Rolfie."

Trish snorted. "It didn't work. She *is* engaged. In fact, she got the ring last week."

Mike groaned. "I never did have much luck. All my life I've been too late. I'm a born loser, I guess."

Trish frowned. She'd never had much patience with whiners.

"You used to take Meg out. What happened? Kix and I were rooting for you."

"I don't know. She did say I was irresponsible— had too many jobs. You know, the old security bit." Mike pounded his right fist into his left hand and said angrily, "Life isn't as serious as some people believe. A fellow should be able to do what he wants to. I never did believe in being nailed to one job—too boring."

Trish nodded in agreement.

174

"Meg was always conservative. She had a lot of responsibility thrust on her when she was seventeen. After our Aunt Martha left because of her arthritis, Meg carried the whole burden. Naturally, she's concerned about our futures."

"You two are pretty well grown-up now," Mike said shortly. "You could support yourselves."

Trish looked at him in amazement. "Meg wants us to go on to college. Of course, we'll work part-time, but—"

The door opened and Meg looked out.

"It's you," she said, and her voice relayed her contempt.

"Meg, let me talk to you for a minute."

"I have nothing to say to you. You think everything is one big, fat joke. Well. . . ." She turned away. Mike leaped to his feet and followed her through the door, closing it behind him.

Trish shook her head and wished she could understand adults. Mike sounded like fun to her, except for the self-pity bit. What if he did have lots of jobs? He made good money. But maybe when you got as old as Meg—twenty-two—you wanted more definite things. As she sat musing, Rolf drove up.

"Oh, great," she said aloud.

"Hello, Trish. I'm back," Rolf said, coming up the walk.

"Meg's talking to Mike Parrish," she volunteered.

Rolf sat down on the porch and sighed. "I thought he got his message across via tape." His tone was dry.

"He's persistent."

Rolf locked his hands across his knees and rocked back and forth. His blond hair fell across his forehead. For the first time, Trish noticed how attractive he was. Having resented him so much in the past, she hadn't observed his good points. His brown eyes were sad.

"Is Meg still upset?"

"I suppose—I haven't talked to her yet."

"She shouldn't take the evening's incidents too seriously. My mother is all surface snootiness; it covers her lack of social confidence. She's the granddaughter of Biddy Doyle, who kept a rooming house, and she has never been able to live that down in her own mind."

Trish looked at him in amazement. "But I thought—" she started.

"Everyone thinks we're landed gentry—but my father made his money himself. *His* father was a bricklayer—a darned good one. Dad had the ad-

176

vantage of college . . . got into banking . . . and, by sheer hard work, long hours, and some courage, became the president of the Morgan City Bank." Rolf chuckled. "Back in Boston, where he started out, we look a little different."

"Sylvia talks as though—"

"Sylvia is a little phony right now. But she's young. Eventually, the good stuff that's in her will surface."

Trish could hardly believe her ears. She finally understood what Meg saw in Rolf. Under his carefully cultivated exterior was a full-blooded human being.

The door wrenched open behind them. Mike stormed out and half ran down the steps, ignoring them completely.

Meg came out and stood looking after him for a moment. Her face wore an odd look. Then she saw Rolf and said, "Oh, hi. Come on in; I'll make some coffee. Join us, Trish?"

They all went into the kitchen. Meg started the coffee. "Was your mother violently angry on the way home?"

"Matter of fact, she was. Not at you but at that goofy dog of yours." He laughed. "Dad said it only proved that the dog loved her at first sight. She

177

sputtered half the way home; then she finally broke down and roared because the whole scene was so insane. Sylvia is still sulking, however. She thinks you planned the whole thing." Rolf looked at Meg for a long moment. "Syl said it was 'psychologically obvious' that you hated me and mine and that you wouldn't ever marry me—engagement or no."

"Imagine—Sylvia saying all that!" Meg grinned slyly. "Such insight—"

"Hah," Trish snorted derisively.

"—and so wrong. I *am* going to marry you, Rolf, in spite of Sylvia, Pushkin, four hamsters, and twenty-four white mice." She reached across the table and took his hand. He grinned at her. Trish yawned mightily as she watched them drink coffee.

A few minutes later, Rolf left. Meg walked him to his car, then came back inside and locked the front door.

They went upstairs companionably. Trish was thinking how amazing it was that a series of events could happen and change your whole way of looking at a person. Rolf had turned human under the most adverse conditions. Amazing.

"Let's say good night to Kix," Meg said. They knocked on her door and entered to find her sitting cross-legged on the bed, leafing distractedly

178

through a pile of magazines. Her eyes were red-rimmed. When she looked at them, her face was forlorn.

"I'm so sorry, Meg. The whole mess was my fault."

"Kix, you're not to brood about it. It happened, and we may as well forget it. Just fix the shelf, once and for all—please!"

"Oh, I will," Kix said fervently. "I'll get Biggie to put screws two inches long into it."

Meg gave Kix a hug.

"What I can't figure is Pushkin. He hates females —except for us. Why did he go ape over Mrs. Creighton?" She sniffed, on the verge of further tears. "If only he hadn't got into the red paint. . . ." Kix's voice trailed off.

Trish visualized the scene again—shaggy Push-kin, dripping red paint, trying to climb on Mrs. Creighton's lap, new suit and all—and exploded into laughter.

Startled, Kix looked at her. Then she, too, started to laugh. Meg joined in.

"That dog," gasped Kix. "Oh, he was too much."

When she had controlled her hysteria somewhat, Trish said, "It certainly was a test by paint for in-laws-to-be. Love Meg, love her dog. And it proved the Creightons aren't so impossible, after all."

"I'm glad nothing was really spoiled for you, Meg," Kix said sleepily. "Guess I'll go to bed."

Meg and Trish walked down the hall to their rooms.

"I was wrong about Mike," Trish said.

"In what way?"

"I thought he was exciting—lots of fun. But now I see that, for the long haul, a man like Rolf will wear better." She gave Meg an impulsive little hug. "Mike has a strong vein of self-pity in him—that would be murder to live with."

Meg smiled. "I'm glad, Trish. I know you favored Mike. And I don't mind admitting I had quite a thing for him. But something told me it wouldn't work out. Rolf and I will help each other. I'll become less anxious about security, and he'll learn to be less inhibited. I know myself, Trish. Rolf is what I want—and need. Mike is for someone much more adventurous."

Trish nodded. Meg said good night and went into her room, closing the door softly. And as Trish prepared for bed, she thought sleepily that the day of mice, hamsters, and red-coated Pushkin had ended well, after all—though for a few minutes there, she wouldn't have given a nickel for the prospective wedding bells which would unite the Dorn and Creighton clans.

With one last wistful thought of Mike, Trish fell asleep—and the house of those Dorn girls was silent at last.

Jessica

Ruth Hooker

JESSICA LAMBERT knew certain things about herself. Her dentist said she had nice teeth and a good "bite." Her best friend was envious of her hair, which was neither blond nor brown but had streaks of both. Her father said she had the clearest blue eyes he'd ever seen. Her mother said Jessica had trim feet, of all things, and a gym teacher once had told her that she was agile.

All these things Jessica, for some reason, had never added up to even a degree of attractiveness. That she was *un*attractive was as certain to Jessica as the coming of dawn.

Jessica also knew that she had a nice personality and a good sense of humor, but she viewed these characteristics as distinct disadvantages. She had formed this opinion after overhearing her cousin and his friends guffawing crudely about the perils of blind dating.

"The worst ones are the ones they say have a, quote, nice personality, unquote."

Another chimed in, "Or how about, quote, a good sense of humor, unquote?" They all had laughed uproariously.

From that exchange, Jessica had formulated a hard and fast rule for herself: Never go on a blind date.

So, with this batch of mistaken premises to build on, Jessica arrived at a conclusion: It was established that no boy would ever date Jessica; conversely, Jessica would never date a boy. Therefore, not only was she sixteen and dateless, but also she would become seventeen and dateless, and so forth, ad infinitum.

Jessica's girl friends accepted the fact that Jessica didn't date. Her mother thought that Jessica simply wasn't interested in boys. Her father still thought of Jessica as his little girl, and the possibility of her dating never crossed his mind. Her little brother couldn't have cared less.

Jessica developed an attitude to protect herself.

It wasn't an *I hate boys* attitude but rather a *Boys?* *Who? Oh, them* posture. It worked very well— perhaps too well. While a little antagonism can be dealt with, there's not much that can be done about indifference.

There was one flaw, though: Jessica really did want to date. No one guessed. No one would have believed it—except Tracy.

Tracy and Jessica shared a gym locker. They were strange locker mates, but then, gym classes breed strange locker mates. Tracy was pert and sure of herself, the most popular girl in school, where boys were concerned. Getting boys to like her was Tracy's main interest, her hobby. She pursued it with enthusiasm and diligence.

The two girls gradually became good friends, at least during gym classes. Jessica felt flattered that someone as popular as Tracy should befriend her. An impartial observer might think it strange that Jessica should befriend a flirt like Tracy. The observer would be wrong, though; there was really quite a bit to Tracy.

Tracy had a certain honesty about her. She never flattered just for flattery's sake. She told Jessica that her clothes were very attractive, which was true. Jessica accepted the compliment easily, because she felt it had nothing to do with her. Jessica's mother was responsible for her tastefully selected wardrobe. When she wore something new, Jessica was sure that the admiring glances were for the garment and not for the girl inside. So, in spite of Tracy's compliment, Jessica's self-esteem remained unaffected.

Tracy never stooped to saying that boys actually were interested in Jessica. Instead, she argued that Jessica could, if she wanted to, make boys take notice of her.

Since Tracy was also generous, she proceeded to share some of her many secrets with Jessica.

At first, Jessica listened with indifference; but after a time, it occurred to her that if she could master math, surely she ought to be able to master Tracy's techniques.

Self-consciously, in her locked bedroom, Jessica began to try new hairstyles, which she immediately brushed out. The many brushings made her hair more lustrous than ever. Then she experimented with cosmetics but usually ended up looking like a clown or a death's-head. It took much scrubbing to erase her efforts, but the scrubbings improved her complexion considerably.

Jessica practiced looking sideways through her

lashes, and she giggled because she looked like an amateur secret agent. She practiced "laughing up into his face" and cringed, because she looked like a plain fool.

Even so, she became more and more intrigued with her experiments and listened more and more attentively to Tracy's advice. Then, early in spring, after a long winter of Tracy's urging Jessica to try her skills on a specific person, Jessica named her first victim. Kurt Tanner, from her geometry class, was chosen—for no special reason other than his seeming a likely choice.

Tracy set to work like a general planning a major campaign.

"Now, what you do," Tracy began, "is just be around when he gets out of class, and you walk in the same direction. Then what you do is bump into him or drop your books or something."

Jessica was aghast. "How about tripping him? That would get his attention."

Tracy had to laugh. "I wouldn't go that far. But do something. It's worth a try."

It took Jessica two days to work up enough nerve to try any attention-getting devices. Finally, though, she convinced herself that she was committed to playing the game. If she never tried, after all, she'd never know. . . .

The very next day, after geometry, Jessica braced herself, held her breath, and dropped her books. The drop was successful—*too* successful. Books flew in every direction, and her loose-leaf notebook's spine sprang open, spreading papers up and down the hall. Not only Kurt Tanner helped pick up papers (two heel-marked ones); everybody else in the hall also fell to, tying up traffic for five minutes and causing general tardiness for the next classes.

When Jessica reported to Tracy in gym, Tracy had to admit that the episode hadn't resulted in exactly a one-to-one relationship.

"Call him up and ask him for the geometry assignment," Tracy suggested.

"But I always know the assignment," Jessica protested.

Tracy convinced her that it didn't matter. "Call anyway. Lose the assignment, or don't get it for once or something—but call!"

That evening, Jessica stewed, did her geometry assignment, chewed her fingernails, repeatedly asked her parents when they were going to walk the dog, and memorized Kurt's phone number.

At last her parents left with the dog. Jessica

clutched the phone and dialed the number. A squeaky-voiced youngster answered.

"Is Kurt there?" she asked shakily.

Squeaky Voice shouted, "Kuuurt. A guuurl. It's a guurl."

From there on, the conversation deteriorated. No, Kurt didn't have the assignment, and gosh, was there one? In the end, Jessica said that she thought maybe she did have it somewhere, and would Kurt like it? He said maybe, but it was kind of late to do geometry, and thanks, anyway.

Jessica drank a glass of milk to calm her nerves.

Jessica decided she was a complete failure, and that was that, but Tracy had a different view. "At least he'll notice you now," she insisted. That was true. Kurt stared at Jessica all through geometry.

The next day, Kurt actually walked down the hall with Jessica—well, not exactly *with* her but sort of nearby. He even said a couple of things. Jessica quickly searched her mind for relevant responses and hit upon "laughing up into his face."

She was executing that maneuver to the best of her ability when she heard a gruff "Hi, Jess." Without looking, Jessica knew who it was. It was Doug, the only person in the whole school who called her

by that name . . . Doug, the neighbor boy from down the street, who just might go home and tell his mother that she was acting absolutely silly and whose mother just might tell her mother.

Jessica chose not to turn his way, not to return his greeting, not even to look at him. Perhaps he would think she was someone else.

Since Jessica had committed herself to learning and applying the skills needed to attract boys, she persevered. By Thursday, Kurt Tanner had spoken to her twice after class. Then, on Friday, he even waited for her and, after commenting on the tough geometry quiz, said, "I'm going to the student center this evening."

Jessica mentally riffled through Tracy's instructions and came up with "act interested." So she said, "How interesting." Then they were separated.

It had been an exhausting week, but by Monday, after a restful weekend, Jessica was willing to go on with her experiment. She wasn't exactly enthusiastic, but she was rather curious to see how it would work out—like a new theorem in geometry. However, it wasn't as clear-cut as geometry. After class, Kurt asked a strange question. "Where were you Friday night, Jessica?"

Jessica had been watching television Friday night, so she told him, "Watching television." Kurt turned and walked away.

Now where was she? Was she attracting him or repelling him? Why? Obviously, there were facets of this operation that she did not understand.

Tracy straightened it out. What Kurt meant, Tracy explained, was that he had wanted Jessica to come to the student center Friday night and meet him there, and when she hadn't shown up, he'd been disappointed. Jessica could hardly believe it. Then, Tracy continued, when Jessica said she had been watching television, that was too much. If Jessica had said baby-sitting or something else that she couldn't have got out of, that wouldn't have been so bad.

"But I *was* watching television," Jessica said.

"Anyway," Tracy insisted, "you're making progress. He is definitely interested. Keep running into him after class. You're doing fine."

Jessica wasn't so sure. She wasn't sure she'd ever learn all the ins and outs of dealing with boys. She wasn't even sure that she wanted to learn. But, with a sigh, she decided to see it through.

For the next two days, she made it a point to

see Kurt after class and say something about geometry—something dumb, because she remembered she shouldn't act too smart in front of boys.

Each day, she'd had to catch up with Kurt, but on Thursday, he waited outside the door with a friend.

"Here comes your shadow now," Kurt's friend said. "Be seeing you."

Jessica was still quivering from that remark, when Kurt said, "I think I ought to tell you—I'm going with a girl from South High."

Nothing in all of Tracy's lessons had prepared Jessica for this. She blushed. She stammered. She said nothing. Turning to flee, she ran smack into Doug.

"Hey, now, Jess. What's your hurry?" Doug asked. Jessica blushed, stammered, and said nothing. She rushed blindly to study hall.

Jessica sat numbly in her seat, with her head bent over her books so that no one would see her face, which was flaming with embarrassment. *How dumb!* Jessica kept saying to herself. Here she was, only sixteen and already the "other woman." How obvious she must have been. "Your shadow," he'd said. *How dumb!* She felt awful. She wanted to die. Maybe she would at least faint, and they'd come with a stretcher and carry her away. And the kids would say, "Poor Jessica; she has some peculiar disease. No wonder she's been acting so strangely."

But she didn't die. She didn't even faint. She just sat there, berating herself, feeling stupid, feeling mal—mal—what was the word? She pulled her dictionary out of her stack of books and opened it to the *m*'s.

There it was. *Maladjusted*. That's what she was, utterly maladjusted. Then her eyes slid down to *maladroit*—"lacking adroitness: inept." Yes, that described her perfectly, Jessica decided. From *maladroit*, she went to the definition of *inept*, and that was even more accurate. It also said, "See *awkward*," which she proceeded to do. That was a still better word, she decided—especially the part about "lacking social grace and assurance." "Causing embarrassment" was also fitting.

There she was: maladjusted, maladroit, inept, and awkward. Somehow it made her feel better to know all that. Now she could face herself and stop pretending she could be different. She resigned herself to her ill fate and managed to live through study hall. She had only one moment of discomfort, when she thought of how she had bumped into Doug. She wondered why that, of all the dumb things she had done recently, bothered her.

In gym class, she made a full confession of the horrible incident to Tracy. Tracy, surprisingly, thought it was a good sign. She insisted that Kurt had only told Jessica about the girl at South High to show that he was a good prospect.

"That settles it," Jessica declared. "I can't do it. Why, I can't even understand the language. I could understand Chinese better than that!"

"Can you understand Chinese?" Tracy asked, believing that Jessica just possibly could.

"No," Jessica told her, "and I certainly can't understand the cryptograms that you and Kurt Tanner use, either."

Tracy looked as impressed by that statement as if it had been Chinese.

Jessica went on. "I quit. I simply can't do it. I'm not the type."

For just a moment, Tracy looked as though she might urge Jessica to reconsider. Then she smiled and shrugged. "Oh, well," she said, "it's probably just as well. If you had made it, you would have been too much competition for me."

Jessica smiled back at her. *No wonder Tracy is popular*, she thought. *She makes people feel good.*

On the way home, alone, Jessica sorted out her thinking of the day. It was quite all right for Tracy, she reasoned, because it suited Tracy. She, though, would never—could never—go out and "get" anyone. She'd just have to wait until some boy came along and made the overtures. He would have to do the choosing. She couldn't. Then it occurred to her that maybe no boy would ever choose her. Well, if that was the case, so be it. She'd just be an old maid. She wondered if her parents would mind terribly having an old maid for a daughter.

That evening, Jessica helped her mother an extra amount, studied extra hard, brushed her hair with extra vigor, and went to bed extra early.

The next morning seemed like a different sort of day. Spring had finally come. Jessica put on her new pale green dress. She dawdled over breakfast. She dawdled at the closet door and finally picked her yellow raincoat.

"You look like a daffodil," her mother told her. "Very perky."

"Thank you," Jessica said and thought to herself, *Who ever heard of a perky old maid?*

Jessica walked slowly, enjoying the fresh and different day. Birds flew about excitedly. The warm, moist wind blew in gusts, rushing the dark clouds along, hiding the sun and then revealing it.

"Jess! Hey, Jess—wait up," a masculine voice called. It was Doug.

Jessica waited while Doug ran with easy strides. "You're late this morning," he said as he drew near. "Usually you're gone before I get back from taking my dad to the station." Then he flushed. "That is . . . I mean . . . I sometimes see you."

Jessica lowered her eyes so as not to cause him more embarrassment, but she peeked at him from between her lashes. He reddened even more. She felt she must change the subject. She looked up at the sky and at the wildly tossing tree branches. "Isn't it an exciting day?" she asked as she turned and looked up at him.

"Yes, it is," Doug agreed—only he wasn't looking at the sky. He was looking at her. Once again, Jessica lowered her eyes. But, once again, she had to peek. This time, Doug looked away, up at the sky.

"Weather is interesting," he said.

"Oh, yes," she agreed. "What's it going to do? Is it going to rain?"

"No," he said, "it's too windy. The wind'll blow all these clouds eastward, and the sun'll come out." At that moment, the sun did come out, as though by command. She laughed up into his face, and he laughed back.

"Say," said Doug, "are you doing anything tonight? I mean—do you have a date with Kurt Tanner or anything? I mean—I see you in the hall with him. You're not going with him or anything, are you?"

Jessica saw him turn red again. *Why, he's just as awkward and maladroit as I am,* she thought. Quickly she said, "Oh, no. Kurt is just in my geometry class. I just talk to him afterward once in a while. That's all."

"Well, great," Doug sighed. "How about it, then?"

"How about what?" she asked demurely, not wanting to be too forward.

"How about going out with me?" he asked.

"I'd like to," she answered. She looked up at him and didn't look away, because he didn't look embarrassed—just happy.

Suddenly Jessica felt happy, too. She knew that Tracy's way with boys would never be her way. But she could develop ways of her own—ways to be well adjusted, adroit, and, most of all, attractive.

The Dollar

Eleanor Roth

You shouldn't be eating cake, Mother. *Especially* not chocolate cake!"

It was a plea more than an admonition, for while her mother had been on that all-too-brief self-improvement spree, the pressures on Sara had eased. But now that her mother had been defeated once again by food, she would be looking for triumphs through Sara.

"I'm too old now." Her mother's voice held a tone of weary acceptance. "I'm just not going to fight anymore." Looking up, her mother let her eyes feast on Sara's slender figure, almost as they feasted on the richly swirled icing on the cake. Sara turned away, beginning to feel choked.

"You've got such a gorgeous shape, Sara. Why can't you dress like a lady?"

Sara didn't answer.

Her mother cut another thin slice of cake. She always cut one tiny slice after another, until half the thing was gone. "You know, the neighbors are *still* talking about the day last week when the youngest Cranston boy drove you home in a Buick half a block long—and where was I?" She shook her head ruefully. "I'd have given my right arm to see the look on Dottie Morgan's face!"

Sara looked down at the floor.

"Okay." Her mother shrugged. "I'm gloating. I admit it. But, honey, can't you understand that I love seeing you have fun and lots of opportunities? *I* never had any chances."

Sara knew the story by heart. She used to cry into her pillow every Christmas when she was little because she'd got a pile of toys and she knew that her mother, the youngest of nine children, had never got anything but a few hand-me-downs.

"Would you believe, Sara, that your father and I used to ride the subway half the night, just to be together, just to be away from our families. . . ."

Her mother's voice took on the richly laden tones of reverie, and Sara listened more closely. "If we felt really well-off because we had an extra few cents between the two of us, we'd take the Staten Island Ferry. But, Sara"—her mother's eyes suddenly sparked resentment—"during the very *worst* times, we never went around the way you kids do, dressed in rags and patches. We always kept up appearances. But you kids seem to want to flaunt something. I don't know. Honey"—her mother's voice turned thin and high with wheedling—"couldn't you just be nice to that young Cranston boy? It would make me so happy."

"I like Ted Cranston a lot, Mom, but I hate using people. And I guess I just don't understand your kind of happiness."

Her mother's back stiffened. "Don't go highfalutin on me, now. You know very well what I mean. I came from nothing; you know that. Don't you understand how good I'd feel if my own daughter went around with real society?" She smiled, and Sara knew she was visualizing Dottie Morgan's face. The dreamlike look vanished as she regarded Sara realistically.

"*Please* don't go out like that. That disgusting work shirt isn't even ironed. Don't disgrace me."

For just a moment, Sara was seeing her mother with fresh eyes, as a stranger might see her. Her face was old and tired-looking. She was fifty-one but looked easily ten years older. With a real sense of sadness, Sara stepped closer to her mother, put her arm around her neck, and kissed her cheek. Suddenly it seemed necessary to show real affection, before it was too late.

"Please take that awful thing off, Sara." Her mother accepted the kiss but let the lovely moment die. "What a world," she sighed. "A pretty young girl wearing her father's oldest threadbare clothes."

"All right, Ma."

She went into her room, took the shirt off, and put on the bright blue blouse her mother had given her last Christmas. With a piece of matching yarn, she tied back her long, straight hair.

She stuck her head into the kitchen. "I'm going out, Ma." Her mother looked at her and nodded appreciatively at the improvement.

It was almost noon when she left the ungainly three-story frame building, which was unaccountably called a "tenement" in this part of New England. She walked toward the mill (now called the "plant") of which Ted Cranston's father was a part owner. The Cranstons wanted their sons to start at the bottom; they felt it was good public relations to show a lack of nepotism. So Ted worked there, in the shipping room, every Saturday morning, and he'd come through the gate as soon as the noon whistle blew.

She heard the low-pitched sound and slowed her pace so she'd be standing directly in front of the gate when he emerged. She would seem to be passing, quite accidentally, on her way to the post office.

She looked away as a whole line of workers spilled out. The line thinned, but Ted didn't appear, and she was glad. She didn't really want to be standing there; she hated feeling like a schemer.

But then he came out. He walked all alone, reading a printed list. He was so engrossed that he didn't even realize she was standing there, until he all but stumbled over her.

"Sara! Hi! What a stroke of luck. I tried to call you last night, but your line was busy—for two hours."

"Oh, Ted, I'm sorry."

"I was feeling low, and I wanted to talk to you, that's all. How've you been?"

"Fine. And you?"

"Aah!" It was a grunt of pure disgust. She drew back as he thrust his fist despairingly through the air. "The whole week's been a bummer."

"Ted—" she stopped and looked at him—"do you want to talk about it now?"

"I sure do! I just wish I had my car. We could've gone for a ride somewhere, and I really could have talked to you. But no, I rode in with my father this morning!"

"Don't worry about that. I live only a couple of blocks from here. Let's go over to my house."

They held hands as they walked. When they reached her block, Sara waited for him to react to the crowded row of clumsy buildings. However, Ted seemed perfectly at ease, though his own home must have been a far cry from surroundings like these.

She rang the bell to their third-floor flat. Her mother didn't come to the door, and Sara was glad that they'd be alone. Unlocking the door, she led him straight into the kitchen, where she took a carton of milk and the rest of the chocolate cake from the refrigerator. Ted was just starting to tell her about his hitchhiking experience that had caused such a family row, when her mother walked in.

"Mother, this is Ted Cranston." She felt almost guilty for enjoying the startled, frozen look on her mother's face.

Ted rose, extending his hand, and her mother stammered something about the mess in the kitchen and moving to the dining room.

"Relax, Ma." Sara smiled.

"Why don't you sit down with us, Mrs. Pearson?" Ted asked. "I was just telling Sara about an experience I had the other day when I hitched a ride home from Boston."

"No, no." Her mother looked embarrassed. "I'll let you kids talk alone."

"Really, Mrs. Pearson, there's no need to go away," Ted repeated.

Looking very unsure of herself, Mrs. Pearson sat down. Only then did she seem to realize what Ted had been saying. "Do *you* hitchhike?" She looked astonished.

"I can see why it seems peculiar to you," Ted admitted. "I guess we do have about five cars in our family. But my father had taken me to Boston, and I didn't want to wait around for him to leave, so I hitched back. Anyway, this middle-aged guy picked me up, and we talked, and the time went fast. Then, when he let me off, he handed me a dollar."

"He handed you a *dollar?*" Sara repeated. Her mother was looking at him as though he'd said,

204

"He handed me the moon."

"You see," Ted explained, "some guys will give a little something to a fellow they've picked up, if they like him and figure he hasn't got anything. Sometimes they'll just say, 'Get yourself a hamburger' or something like that."

Mrs. Pearson glanced at Ted's torn jeans. "And the way you all dress nowadays, no one could tell whether one of you kids was rich or starving."

Ted nodded, and Mrs. Pearson smiled. Sara had wondered at Ted's willingness to have her mother share their conversation, but now she began to feel relaxed. Turning to Ted, she asked, "But you accepted it?"

"Well, you know, he really took me by surprise. I had just said, 'Thanks for the ride,' so when he handed me the dollar, the most natural thing was to say 'Thanks again'—instead of fumbling for an explanation of why he needed it more than I did and embarrassing him. Anyway, I didn't have much time to think about it. Before I could decide what to do, he'd zoomed off."

Her mother shrugged. "I can understand that easily enough."

Sara was glad that they were sitting in the kitchen. Her mother didn't feel out of place in her old housedress, because Sara and Ted were both wearing jeans, and the kitchen smells were reassuring. Then, as Sara watched her searching for the words to express her feelings, she knew that her mother had stopped seeing Ted solely as a person who represented thousands of dollars.

"I can understand why you took it, Ted." Mrs. Pearson nodded. "I know what it's like, having to accept things and wanting to say no to some but not knowing how."

"What do you mean, Ma?"

"There's no great mystery, Sara." Her mother looked from her to Ted and back. "It just feels awkward to refuse an offer of help when someone's genuinely interested in you. After he's been nice, you're really afraid of hurting his feelings or, like you said"—she turned to Ted—"making him feel embarrassed. Besides, no one can know *exactly* how bad off you are. So maybe he misjudged and figured you're worse off than you are, but he *meant* well. Anyway, he did you a favor when he gave you the ride. It's hard to make distinctions—to say, 'Look, mister, I needed this, but I don't need that.' It's a lot easier to just be as—as—"

"Gracious, Ma?" Sara volunteered.

"I guess that's it. To accept a thing as graciously

as it was offered. Not fight it or make a big thing out of it—just say thanks."

"Boy," Ted muttered. "You sure make it sound simple. You're just about the only person who understands it at all." Ted shook his head. "I guess accepting the dollar wasn't my big mistake. It was being fool enough to tell my father about it!"

"But why did you?" Sara asked.

"I wish I knew."

"How did your father react?" Mrs. Pearson asked.

"He was furious! 'What do you think you're doing—accepting money from a stranger?'" Ted imitated his father's righteous anger. "'That guy worked for his money. What did you do to earn it?'"

"Your father didn't understand anything about feelings of friendship?" Sara asked.

"Are you kidding? He just felt ridiculous and humiliated. After all, he's a rich man, and his son accepted a dollar, like a beggar."

"You didn't *ask* for it." Mrs. Pearson was emphatic. "Beggars have no pride. You didn't want to embarrass the man. You were just being kind."

"I don't know what I was being. I just know that I didn't refuse it." Ted looked miserable. "Anyway, things have been lousy at home."

He looked very young and very forlorn, and Sara saw a look of compassionate understanding cross her mother's face, as though she understood quite clearly why some strange man in a genial mood had offered Ted a dollar.

"My parents had such hopes for me and my brother." Ted sighed. "Well, they sure are disappointed. They never had much of anything themselves, you know."

"Really?" Sara practically choked on her last bite of cake. "Really, Ted? Your parents were poor?"

"If they were poor," her mother said pensively, "they should have understood about the dollar."

"Well, they say they were poor, but I guess they weren't *that* poor. Anyway, after they made their pile, they swore their kids would have every opportunity they'd missed."

Mrs. Pearson's eyes narrowed, and she listened intently as Ted went on. "My father had to struggle through college, so he made it easy for us. Only —I don't know. Maybe my brother and I don't even belong in college. Or maybe the constant harping about the importance of an education has made us uptight about not measuring up. Anyway, we *haven't* measured up, that's for sure."

He stared disconsolately at his empty glass, and Sara said, "Gosh, Ted, I'm sorry things are like that."

"I understand how your folks feel," her mother said quietly. "But parents can't live through their kids."

Sara looked up sharply, wondering if she'd heard right. Sure, her mother could see that Ted's parents wanted to realize their ambitions through their kids, but hadn't *she* been doing exactly the same thing?

As Sara watched her mother's face, she had a feeling of elation. Her mother was actually relating to her and Ted. For the very first time, she was viewing the world through their eyes. As Sara stared at her mother, the woman's wrinkles seemed to soften. Even her eyes seemed brighter and younger.

And then the doorbell rang. They hadn't locked the door, and Sara felt crushed at Dottie Morgan's unannounced intrusion into this very precious moment of their lives.

"Oh—you have a *guest?*" Dottie stared at Ted appraisingly. "I didn't see any car. The last time Sara brought a guy home, she made some swell impression around here, let me tell you!"

Sara signaled warnings to both Ted and her mother as she replied, "You didn't see a car, Dottie, because we walked."

"Oh, he doesn't have a car." Dottie nodded, rephrasing Sara's statement. She turned to Ted. "Do you live around here?"

"I live about ten miles away," he told her.

"But you work in town."

Sara and her mother smiled as they shared a meaningful look, a comforting expression between two people who understood each other. *We don't owe this busybody any explanations,* it secretly proclaimed. And, more important: *Ted's one of us. We won't flaunt his family to impress anyone; we won't use a friend to feed our little egos.*

Sara's heart filled with pride as her mother spoke. "Yes, Dottie. Ted works right here in town. In the mill."

"In the *plant*," Sara corrected her, smiling.

"That's right, in the plant," Ted agreed.

Acknowledgments

"NOT MANY GIRLS PLAY FIRST BASS" by Lael J. Littke; "A DIFFERENT KIND OF KNOWING" by Kay Haugaard; "BOYS ARE LIKE ALGEBRA" by Audrey DeBruhl; "SUNDAY'S CHILD" by Audrey DeBruhl; "SECOND BEST" by Willie Mary Kistler; "PROMISE NOT TO TELL" by Mary Knowles. Previously unpublished. Permission of the authors and Larry Sternig Literary Agency.

"THE DOLLAR" by Eleanor Roth; "THOSE DORN GIRLS" by Dorothy Dalton. Previously unpublished. By permission of the authors and Ray Peekner Literary Agency.

"SIGNALS" by Betty Ren Wright. Copyright © 1973 by Ingenue Communications, Inc. Reprinted by permission of the author and Larry Sternig Literary Agency.

"JESSICA" by Ruth Hooker. Previously unpublished. Published by permission of the author.

"DADDY IS A LITTLE DOLL" by Constance Kwolek. Previously unpublished. Published by permission of the author.